Also by Deborah Ellis

Looking for X

The Breadwinner

Parvana's Journey

Mud City

A Company of Fools

The Heaven Shop

Three Wishes: Palestinian and Israeli Children Speak

*Our Stories, Our Songs: African Children
Talk About AIDS*

I AM A
TAXI

The

Cocalero ✳ ✳ ✳ ✳ ✳ ✳ ✳ ✳

Novels

I AM A
TAXI

❋ ❋ ❋ ❋ ❋ ❋ ❋ ❋ ❋ ❋ ❋

Deborah Ellis

Groundwood Books
House of Anansi Press
Toronto Berkeley

Groundwood Books / House of Anansi Press
110 Spadina Avenue, Suite 801, Toronto, Ontario M5V 2K4
Distributed in the USA by Publishers Group West
1700 Fourth Street, Berkeley, CA 94710

We acknowledge for their financial support of our publishing program the
Canada Council for the Arts, the Government of Canada through the
Book Publishing Industry Development Program (BPIDP) and the
Ontario Arts Council.

ONTARIO ARTS COUNCIL
CONSEIL DES ARTS DE L'ONTARIO

Library and Archives Canada Cataloging in Publication
Ellis, Deborah
I am a taxi / by Deborah Ellis
(The cocalero novels)
ISBN-13: 978-0-88899-735-7 (bound).–
ISBN-10: 0-88899-735-3 (bound).–
ISBN-13: 978-0-88899-736-4 (pbk.) –
ISBN-10: 0-88899-736-1 (pbk.)
1. Coca industry – Bolivia – Juvenile fiction. 2. Bolivia – Juvenile
fiction. I. Title. II. Series: Ellis, Deborah, Cocalero novels.
PS8559.L5494I17 2006   jC813'.54   C2006-902814-1

Printed and bound in Canada

To those we keep in cages

CHAPTER ONE

December 31, 1999

"You're wasting your time," Mamá said.

Diego looked around the tiny cell. Clothes and blankets were all piled together on the floor. Nothing could be left behind. They'd need every one of their few belongings to get started again in their new life.

He spied Corina's rag doll, momentarily abandoned while his three-year-old sister crawled under the bed to chase a ball of wool that had rolled away from their mother. In a flash, he tucked it into the pile.

A screech from her told him he hadn't moved

quickly enough. She dove in, looking for her toy and messing up his work.

"No, Corina, leave that there." Diego tried to pull his sister away from the pile, but she screeched again.

"Shut up!" yelled the crabby woman from the cell beside them.

Diego dropped his sister's arm. She shut up, giving him the defiant little smile she wore when things went her way.

"Give her the doll," Mamá said.

"But everything will go faster if I pack it now."

"Give her the doll," Mamá repeated. "I don't want to be knitting for nothing again."

Mamá knit to make money to buy food and pay rent on their cell. If Corina made too much noise or Diego misbehaved, Mamá had to appear before the Prison Discipline Committee. That meant paying a fine or doing an extra chore.

Diego wanted to say it didn't matter if they got fined. In a very short time they'd be out of there, far away from the prison, back to their bit of land where Corina could scream her lungs out among the coca bushes and no one would say anything. But he didn't. He reached into the pile and pulled out the doll.

Corina grabbed the rag toy out of his hands and turned her back on him.

Oh, yes, be mad at me, Diego thought. Stay mad, for years and years. Stay mad and don't bother me.

He took another look around the cell. The narrow bed they all shared took up most of the space. That's where his mother now sat, her multi-layered pollera skirts and petticoats spread out around her. It annoyed him that she looked so calm, her long dark braids hanging smoothly against her shoulders.

"Is there anything left to pack?"

"Your common sense," Mamá said, clicking away on her knitting needles. Mamá knit from morning to night, sometimes not even stopping to eat.

"Why not pack your knitting now and save time later?" Diego asked, without any hope that she'd actually take his suggestion. He got the old raised eyebrow for an answer. The needles kept clicking.

Diego gave up. He only hoped she'd move fast

enough when the time came. Corina he could carry, even if she was squawking and fighting him. He wouldn't have to carry her far. Just a few steps.

He bound up the pile of belongings in an aguayo and tied all the corners together. Could he carry it *and* his sister? He hefted the bundle over his shoulder, then bent down and grabbed Corina. She kicked and swung at him, hitting him in the face with her doll.

He could manage both. He put Corina back down.

"I'm going to say goodbye to the place," he said. He had too much energy tonight to stay in the cell. It was against the rules for children to be out of their mothers' cells at night, but this was New Year's Eve, and some of the rules were relaxed. "But don't worry – I won't get into trouble."

"See that you don't," Mamá said.

Diego popped his head back in the cell.

"Don't go to sleep," he said.

"I won't."

"Promise me?"

His mother looked up at him and smiled. "I promise. But you're wasting your time."

Diego darted out again. There was no point

arguing with his mother, and if he hung around, Corina might forget she was angry with him and insist she go with him.

Diego's mother had a cell on the second floor of the San Sebastián Women's Prison, where women arrested in Bolivia's Altiplano came to serve their sentences. Officially the prison only had two floors, but the place was so full of women and children that more cells had been built on top of and behind the regular cells. The cell Diego shared with his mother and sister was tucked in behind other cells. This cushioned it a bit from the noise, but made it hard for a fresh breeze to find them in the summer.

Diego reached the balcony and hung over the railing. As always, drying laundry stretched from one balcony to the next. Some of the prisoners earned money by doing laundry for people on the outside. Diego looked between the rows of clothes and sheets. Below, the courtyard was busy. The guards were relaxed, letting people enjoy the holiday. Some guards bent over plates of beans, rice and plantain, prepared at one of the prisoner-run restaurants. Diego was sure they hadn't paid. Guards never paid.

Women with bundles passed by him, heading for the staircase. Diego leaned farther over the railing so he could see the entranceway.

It was packed! More than two hours to go until New Year's Eve, and women and children were already lining up at the door.

In a flash, he was back in his mother's cell.

"Come on!" he urged. "They're gathering at the main door. We have to go down there and get a space if we're going to get through. The doors will be open for only five minutes!" He picked up the bundle and lunged for his sister, but she scurried under the bed.

"Diego, that's enough," his mother said. "The doors are not going to open. Things like that don't really happen. And if they did happen, they wouldn't happen to people like us."

"Maybe not usually," Diego said. "But tonight is different. It's the new millennium. You've heard people talking. At midnight, the Angel Gabriel is going to unlock the prison doors everywhere, and keep them open for five minutes. Not even the strongest guards will be able to shut them, and then —"

"Every prisoner who can get through those

doors in those five minutes will be free," Mamá finished for him. "It's not going to happen, and I don't want you to be disappointed."

Diego knelt before his mother and put his hands on hers to stop her knitting.

"But what if it does?" he asked. "What if the Angel Gabriel *does* really come to Cochabamba and opens the doors, and we're not there?"

His mother smoothed the hair out of Diego's eyes.

"And how do you suppose the Angel Gabriel can go to all the prisons in the whole world in the same night, in the same moment?"

"He's the Angel Gabriel, isn't he? What's the point of being an angel if you can't open a few prison doors?"

Mamá looked at him for a long moment. Then she said, "Corina, come out from under the bed. We're going downstairs to wait for the Angel Gabriel."

Once his mother decided to move, she moved fast. The knitting was put away, Corina was hauled out from under the bed, and within minutes, they were headed out of the cell.

Mamá went first with Corina. Diego followed

with the bundle. He stopped in the doorway and took one final look at what had been his home for nearly four years. It was small and dark, a naked bulb hanging from the low ceiling their only light — when the power was working. He could cross the cell in five steps.

He'd grown in four years, but the cell hadn't. He wouldn't miss it. What was there to miss?

He hurried after his mother, past the cell where the crabby woman lived, past the cell with the woman who cried all the time, and down the dark, narrow staircase to the courtyard.

Mrs. Sanchez waved them over. She wore blue jeans, not traditional clothes, and had been the first woman to be kind to them when they arrived at the prison. She was there for killing her husband, but that didn't stop Diego from liking her.

"I've saved you a spot," she said, moving her bundles so Diego and his family could sit on the floor behind her.

The courtyard was filling up quickly. Diego counted ten families ahead of his. He couldn't see behind him clearly enough to count the people who were there. They didn't concern him, unless they moved a lot faster than his mother and sister and pushed them out of the way.

"We'll have to stick together," Diego said. "Mamá, maybe you should go first, with Corina. I'll be right behind you with our things." It might be safer to push his sister than pull her. If she got mad later, he could claim someone else had shoved her.

"Papá is going to meet us by the fountain," Diego reminded his mother. "I hope he's packed and ready. I hope he's in line already."

"Don't you worry about your father," Mamá said. "If there's a way out of prison tonight, he'll find it."

"And what about after that?" Mrs. Sanchez asked. "What will you do when you meet up?"

"We'll go back to our farm," Diego said. He knew it wasn't really their farm. They just lived on it and worked on it, but it felt like theirs. "Papá thinks the house will need some repairs since it hasn't been looked after for so long. I'll help him with that. Mamá will pull the weeds from the garden, and plant beans and potatoes, and Corina..." It was hard to imagine what Corina would do. She'd never seen the farm. "Corina will stop annoying me," he said finally.

"Keep that line straight," Guard López bellowed out, her sharply pressed green uniform in contrast to the rumpled clothes of the prisoners. "People still need to pass by, and I don't want any problems."

"Guard López," he asked her, "you won't try to stop us tonight, will you?"

"No, Diego, we won't," Guard López replied. "But we don't like it one bit. Our job is to keep prisoners in, not let them out. But we have orders from the Bureau of Prisons in La Paz not to interfere with the Angel Gabriel."

"See, Mamá? Even the government thinks we'll get out tonight."

"The government has been wrong before," Mamá said, but softly.

"You have a fine son," the guard said. "Always polite. How old is he now? Nine?"

"Twelve," Mamá said.

"Nearly thirteen," Diego said.

"Prison children are always small for their age." Guard López shouted out to the whole line. "When midnight comes, there will be order at this gate! Anyone who shoves will be yanked out of line, and you'll lose your chance at freedom."

Mamá took out her knitting and settled down to wait. Corina crawled into Mamá's lap, sucking on her doll's foot. Diego was disgusted, but at least she was quiet.

Not all the women in the prison were lining up to get out. Some had opened their little shops and restaurants around the courtyard. Diego smelled onions frying. A woman he often ran errands for was sitting by her big sack of coca leaves, hoping for customers. Other prisoners were hanging over the balcony, looking down at the scene below.

"Here he comes! I see the angel!" one of them jeered.

"You think things are any better out there?" another one called.

Diego looked up at them, then realized something.

"Mamá," he said, "we're sitting in the same spot where we slept when we first came here!"

Four years ago, Corina hadn't been born yet, and Diego was only eight. He and his mother slept on a mat in the courtyard for the first year because Mamá didn't have enough money to rent a cell.

Diego closed his eyes. If he tried hard, he could still imagine the feel of the wind, cool and soft as it came down from the mountains. The green of the farm was so deep he could almost taste it. He'd helped to plant their small vegetable garden, plunged his fingers into the good, dark earth, and gathered eggs from their chickens. Up the hill from their small stone house were their coca bushes, whose little green leaves they chewed when food ran low, and sold for money for clothes and Diego's school books.

But the good memories were always pushed aside by the one bad memory – the day when everything changed.

Diego and his parents had been riding the trufti to the Saturday market in Arani with other farmers, to sell their vegetables and dried coca leaves. The man across the aisle had a bag that kept squirming. He let Diego look at the guinea pigs inside. Diego was so absorbed in stroking their soft fur, he didn't notice that the police had stopped the minibus until his arm was grabbed and he was dragged off.

Deborah Ellis

People and vegetables everywhere, chickens flapping out of banged-open cages, sacks of coca ripped open, the leaves swirling over the ground like green snow. For a long and terrible moment, Diego couldn't find his parents. Then his father found him, and everything was okay again.

But not for long. Small packets of coca paste were found taped under the seat where Diego's family was sitting. It wasn't their paste, but they were arrested anyway. His mother ended up in San Sebastián Women's Prison in Cochabamba. His father was across the square in the men's prison.

"Ten minutes to go!" someone called out. Diego opened his eyes. Everyone stood.

"Come on, Mamá, put the knitting away!" Diego picked up the bundle and tried to move forward.

"No shoving!" the guards yelled.

Diego helped his mother stand up. Corina had fallen asleep and was dead weight in her mother's arms.

Around him, women started praying the rosary. Others sang "Ave Maria."

"Thirty seconds!" someone yelled.

I Am a Taxi 21

The crowd moved forward.

Then, "Twenty seconds!"

"Goodbye, prison!" someone yelled.

"Ten, nine, eight, seven!" Diego joined in counting down the seconds. "Three! Two! One!"

The crowd surged forward again. But only a little.

The prison doors did not open.

"Maybe the time is wrong," someone suggested.

The guards were laughing. One of them flipped on the radio in the guard station and turned up the volume.

All of Bolivia was celebrating the New Year. "Welcome to the year 2000!" the announcer exclaimed. "Happy New Year!"

Still, the doors didn't open.

"I guess the Angel Gabriel passed you by," one of the guards said. "Party's over. Go back to your cells." They herded the prisoners out of the courtyard.

"Are you all right?" Mamá asked Diego quietly.

Diego wiped his eyes. "Papá is probably out in the park, waiting for us by the fountain," he said. "The Angel probably didn't know there are two San Sebastián prisons in Cochabamba."

"Then we can be happy for your father. And we can go to bed."

It took awhile to get all the women, their children and their bundles up the little staircase. Diego heard some of them crying. He just felt numb.

"Unpack tomorrow," Mamá said. "Sleep now."

The three of them climbed onto the narrow single bed. Corina went against the wall so she couldn't get out without Mamá knowing. Then Mamá went in the middle, and Diego on the outside.

It took a long time for the prison to get quiet that night. Women were crying, and some were fighting with the guards. The night was all sobs and screams and anger.

Diego slept, but woke up a few hours later. His mother was crying, very quietly.

"Madre de Dios," she prayed, "how will we survive?"

Diego kept still, so she wouldn't know he'd heard her.

CHAPTER TWO

April, 2000

"Taxi!"

Diego's feet took him out of the cell before his ears were completely sure what he'd heard. The thing to do was to move fast. He couldn't run on the steps – that would mean a fine for his mother from the prison committee – so he walked down them as quickly as he could.

He made it to the bottom floor, and now he could run. He wove past the shopkeeper who sold biscuits and around the plastic tables where some inmates were eating.

"Taxi!" Diego heard it again.

In the next instant, he was standing in front

Deborah Ellis

of Mrs. Morales. Two other boys got there almost at the same time. They were fast, but not quite as fast as he was!

"Diego, you are here first, so you get the job." She handed him a letter. "Take this to the post office. It's to my brother in Canada. Bring me back a receipt, and I'll pay you one Boliviano."

"The post office is quite far," Diego said. There were no fixed rates for jobs, but after years of being a taxi, he knew what a task was worth.

"Two Bolivianos," Mrs. Morales conceded. "But bring back a receipt or you get nothing. How will I know you didn't throw the letter away and spend the money on candy?" She handed Diego fifteen Bolivianos to pay for the stamp and waved him on his way.

Diego was slightly insulted by that remark. He was not a child, wasting money on frivolous things. He was nearly a man, and he had a family to support. Mrs. Morales should know by now that he could be trusted.

Word traveled fast in a world as small as a prison.

"You're going out?" gentle old Mrs. Álvarez asked him. She'd been arrested after a lodger at her house had hidden coca paste in her shed. "You will light a candle for me in the cathedral?"

"Of course, Mrs. Álvarez," he said, accepting her fifty-centavo coin for the candle. She asked him to do this almost every day. He never charged her for these trips. Sometimes it was good business to do things for free, although he always wanted to tell her to save her money. All the candles she had lit, and she was still in prison.

Diego put the money and letter away in his special pocket. His mother had made one of his pockets very deep, so things wouldn't fall out, and so thieves could not rob him in the street. Fifteen Bolivianos was a lot of money. It could buy them two days' worth of bread and fruit. But he wasn't tempted to keep it, not even for a minute. His mother would have to pay Mrs. Morales back, and he would be finished as a taxi. For half a day he'd be rich, but poor forever after that.

He went up to the first door to get out – one of the two doors that the Angel Gabriel had failed to open on New Year's Eve. The guards on duty had worked there for years and barely acknowledged him as he went through the door.

But between that door and the outside door was a small foyer, with a desk and another guard. This guard was new.

"Who are you?" she asked, without a smile.

Who are *you*? Diego wanted to ask in return, but he'd learned long ago that guards were always right, especially when they weren't.

"My name is Diego. My mother is Drina Juárez."

He waited while she looked his mother's name up in the prison records. It took a long time, because she wasn't really sure where to look.

Finally, she found it. "And what do you want?"

"I am a taxi," he said.

"You want me to get you a taxi? That is certainly not part of my job."

"No, I *am* a taxi." He dug the letter out of his deep pocket, careful not to spill the money onto the floor. "I have an errand to run for Mrs. Morales."

The guard took the letter, held it up to the light, squeezed it, ruffled it between her hands.

"I don't know," she said.

"It's just a letter. I do this all the time," Diego blurted out. He should have held his tongue, but how much nonsense could he be expected to take?

The guard frowned, kept her grip on the letter and went to the inner door to call another guard.

"This boy says he's going to mail a letter."

The guard who was summoned had been at the prison as long as Diego and had let him pass many times without even a lifted eyebrow. Still, guards had to stick together. Diego was questioned on who had given him the letter and what he was supposed to do with it, until finally, as if bestowing a great favor, he was given the letter back and allowed to go through the final door.

"I'm not a prisoner," he muttered, once he was safely outside. "You can't boss me around."

It was a relief to be on the good side of the prison walls for the first time in more than a week. Protests over who controlled Cochabamba's water had shut down the whole city, including the schools, with campesinos coming from all over the district to take over the streets. The prison was shut for security reasons, and because a lot of the guards couldn't make it in to work. Diego had to miss all the excitement. It felt good to be outside again.

The schools were still closed while the remains of the barricades were cleared from the streets, so Diego had the whole day to himself.

He looked around quickly. He wasn't noticing the flowers blooming in the park in the middle of the square, or the water from the fountain sparkling in the morning sunlight. He was too busy looking for friends and enemies.

He didn't look closely enough. No sooner had he taken a few steps away from the prison than he was surrounded by one of the gangs of older boys who roamed the city with nothing to do but make trouble for hard-working kids like Diego. Diego recognized them. They usually hung out at one of the video game cafés up near the Plaza Quintanilla. They had bothered him before. They weren't really dangerous, just bored, but Diego wished they would find some other amusement.

"What's in your hand? Anything you'd like to share with us?"

One of the guys snatched the letter out of

Diego's hand. He held it upside down, pretending to read it.

Diego reached for the letter, but the gang passed it around, too high and too fast for him to get hold of it again. He blamed the new guard. If she hadn't kept him waiting so long, he'd have remembered to put the letter back in his pocket. At least his money was safe.

"Give me my letter!" he yelled, even though he knew it would do no good.

Something pushed at the biggest kid from behind. Then another kid was pushed the same way. Diego's letter floated down to him. He grabbed it and ran.

"Saved you again," his best friend, Mando, said as they darted in and out of traffic. "That makes ten thousand times that I've saved your life."

"Not ten thousand," Diego corrected, yelling over his shoulders. "More like eight thousand." He checked to see if they were being followed, but the older boys were too lazy to run, unless they were chasing a sure thing or running from the police. "Plus, I've saved you a few thousand times, too, so you're not that much up on me."

Mando, short for Armando, was thin and wiry, at least a head taller than Diego. Diego didn't think he'd ever seen his friend being still. Every part of his body always seemed to be moving.

Mando's mother was dead. He lived with his father in the men's prison. Unlike Diego's parents, Mando's father really had tried to smuggle coca paste, to get the family out of the debt they had run up trying to pay for his mother's medical bills.

"Did you see what I did?" Mando asked, dancing and weaving down the sidewalk. "In and out. Move in fast, zoom out of the way. That's what boxers do."

"So now you're a boxer?" Diego asked. "I thought you were going to be a race car driver."

"You need money to be a race car driver. I'll be a famous boxer first. Then people will buy me cars to race and won't care if I smash them, because it will be such an honor for them to have me smash up their cars."

"I'm going to the post office," Diego said. "Where are you off to?"

"The market," said Mando. "One of the cooks wants potatoes. Then I've got to deliver some sandals. Coming to watch the football game later?"

"I'll see how the day goes."

"Okay, big shot, big tycoon. Soon you'll do your errands in one of those big fancy cars with the dark windows."

"When I get one of those cars, I'll hire you to do my errands. You'll have to work hard, or I won't pay you."

In response, Mando tried to throw Diego into the fountain. Then Diego tried to throw Mando into the fountain, but it was a work day, so they put a stop to the fooling around, and went to work.

The post office wasn't really that far from the prison, but Mrs. Morales was from Potosí and didn't know Cochabamba at all. Besides, her relatives sent her money. She could afford to pay him an extra Boliviano.

With his conscience clear, Diego broke into a jog and ran the whole length of the square. He ran by the corner of the square where chairs, bed frames and dog houses made in the woodworking shop of the men's prison were stacked. He ran past the old Aymara woman selling saltenas from a charcoal-heated stand, and he ran by the dogs who lived in the park. The dogs were too sleepy in the sunshine to even look up as he ran by.

The streets and sidewalks were more crowded than usual. Many of the campesinos had gone back to their villages after the protest, but others were still in the city, celebrating their victory over the big companies that wanted to take over Cochabamba's water.

"Hey, my friend," an old man called to Diego, raising a box of chicha in the air in a salute. "Come join our party. Bolivian water for Bolivian thirsts!"

"That's not water you're drinking," Diego said with a grin.

"No, but this is also for Bolivian thirsts!"

Diego waved and kept going. It would be wonderful to sit and listen to stories of the blockade, but he had work to do.

Diego tried to find the least crowded of the streets. He turned up Avenida Ayacucho, past the movie house where *Batman* was playing, and four blocks later he was at the post office.

"I need a receipt," he said to the teller.

"Please," she said.

"Please," Diego said with a grin. The woman behind the counter smiled back and handed him his receipt. He put it carefully into his deep pocket.

To be a taxi was to always be on the lookout – for dangers and opportunities. The world was full of chances to make a few Bolivianos. It was also full of people who wanted to take those Bolivianos away. Diego kept his eyes open and headed toward the cathedral to light Mrs. Álvarez's candle.

The cathedral was a few blocks across town, on the Plaza 14 de Septiembre. The plaza was a very grand place, with covered walkways all around it, and gardens that were larger and better cared for than the ones in Plaza San Sebastián.

Another celebration was going on in front of the cathedral, with musicians blowing into the long reeds of the sanka and drumming away on the bombo. Diego heard fragments of a speech a woman was giving as he turned into the cathedral. "Today we will burn our water bills," she said. "Bolivian water belongs to Bolivian people!"

Deborah Ellis

Mass was coming to an end up by the main altar. Diego lit a candle for Mrs. Álvarez at a side altar to St. Peter and watched the nuns behind the grill talk quietly with visitors. He liked the cathedral. It was clean and quiet.

A lot of prisoners needed a taxi that day. After giving Mrs. Morales her receipt, he went out again to buy some tomatoes and onions for one of the inmates who operated a little diner in the prison, and to pick up something at the drug store for someone else. When he got back from those trips, his mother sent him out for wool.

"Get used if you can, new if you have to, and if you have to buy new, go to the stall by the coca market, not the shop down the street."

Diego knew. He'd gone on wool runs often enough. On his way out, he was asked by the woman who sold coca leaves to other prisoners to replenish her supply.

"Go to the woman who sold them to you last time. They were a good quality."

More money went into his pockets. He kept track of the amounts in his head. So much for wool, so much for coca, so much was his pay from the jobs he had already done. He didn't need to carry a notebook to write things down. The notebook in his head kept track of everything just fine.

The second-hand clothing market was first, and Diego was lucky. He found two old sweaters, torn and dirty but made with the right kind of wool. One was yellow and one was pale green. His mother would wash them, unravel them, then knit something new with the wool.

In the coca market, merchants dished out small packets of dried coca leaves from the big sacks in front of them. Diego didn't remember very much about growing coca, but he liked talking to the merchants as though he shared their knowledge of working the soil and pruning the branches. He wasn't just a prison boy. He was a cocalero.

He asked about villages and rainfall as he wound his way through the women in woolen shawls and bowler hats and the men with their cheeks puffed out, full of coca leaves. Deep in the market, he found the merchant he was looking for.

"Compliments on your coca," he said in Quechua to the old woman surrounded by sacks

Deborah Ellis

of the little green leaves. "The women in San Sebastián like it very much." He told her how much he wanted to buy.

Instead of measuring out the leaves, she looked at him with practiced eyes.

"You are an honest boy?"

"I am a taxi," he said. "I am a good business-man, and being honest is good business."

"Then I have a job for you." She gave him a parcel of leaves. "Take this to the American consulate. Their people have been warned to stay inside because of the protests and I know they will soon run out of coca leaves for their tea. They pay well, and I want to keep them as customers. Here is the address." She wrote it down on a slip of paper. "Do you know how to get there?"

"It's on the same road as the university," he said. "No, don't pay me now. Pay me when I bring back your money."

"Good business," the merchant nodded. "Let the gringo women see how cute you are. They'll give you a big tip. I will hold your bundle for you until you get back."

Diego handed over the sweaters he'd bought

for his mother and headed off quickly. The fastest way out was through the witchcraft market, full of herbs, good-luck charms, and yatiri telling fortunes. In and out of the stalls he wove, until finally he came out into the open air, where the bread sellers were competing with cars and minibuses.

The American consulate was high up in a new building. Diego felt the scruffiness of his clothes as he walked into the shiny, clean entranceway. He wondered if the city dust on his shirt would lessen his tip. There was an elevator, but he wasn't sure he was allowed on it, so he took the stairs instead, after checking on the sign for the right floor. The steps were clean and bright and wide.

At the right floor, he left the staircase. The hall was also bright, and at the end was a double set of glass doors with two guards with guns standing in front. Diego saw the American flag through the glass and knew he was at the right place.

"I have a delivery," he said to the guards, who didn't reply. He tried to go in, but the doors wouldn't open. A voice came out of nowhere and spoke to him in English. It had to repeat itself before Diego thought to reply.

"I have coca leaves," he said in Spanish, holding up the package so they could see through the door.

The first set of doors clicked open. Two more very tall men in uniforms and no smiles motioned to Diego to put his package on a moving belt. It went through a machine while they frowned at it. Diego had to walk through a doorway beside the machine – a doorway that didn't really go anywhere. Finally, he got his package back and was allowed to go through the second set of doors and into the consulate.

A blonde woman in a clean and pressed light blue dress greeted him. He gave her the leaves.

"The merchant said you might be running low," he said in Spanish. He hoped she understood this was business, not a gift.

"I have a little boy just your age," she said, smiling kindly. Her fingernails were shiny and pink. Diego thought about his mother's nails, cracked and worn down from hard work.

The American woman paid him – plus a good tip – and he left the consulate.

Just outside the glass doors were posters of American cities – San Francisco, with the long bridge over blue water, New York City crowded with buildings, and some place with an endless beach. Diego wondered briefly if the cities he was looking at had prisons. Then he was on his way again.

After all, he was a taxi, and a taxi needed to keep moving.

CHAPTER THREE

﹡

Diego headed back through the market. The coca seller was pleased to see him. She told him to keep his tip for himself and added her own delivery payment. Then he paid for the coca and for two hunks of legia – one sweet and one salty. Legia was the chalky paste that people chewed to help draw the juice from the coca leaves. He asked for a written note of the price. He never wanted anyone to question his honesty. Cheating was bad, bad business.

He picked up his bundle of coca and the sweaters for his mother and headed home. The food sellers were putting more coal on their grills to make them hot enough to cook all the food they would need for their evening customers.

Scents of grilling meat from anticuchos, of hot oil on fried potatoes, and of smoked corn husk filled the air around Diego, reminding him that he hadn't eaten all day.

He fingered the Bolivianos in his pocket. His mother didn't mind if he spent his earnings on food for himself. "Eat and be strong," she always said. The grilled sausages and milanesa were tempting, but he knew the chupe was more filling, and cheaper.

He bought a bowl of chupe and sat down at a table to eat it. The soup was thick with grains and tomatoes. He even found bits of meat among the potatoes. He didn't realize how hungry he was until he started eating. He shoveled the soup in without stopping until the bowl was empty.

"A boy who likes to eat. Very nice," the chupe seller said, as she put his bowl and spoon in a bucket to wash.

Diego sat for a moment to let the food settle, and to catch his breath after eating so fast. He knew the market well by now. He loved its rhythms of people doing business and getting what they needed, and being tired at the end of a day of doing things well.

When he first started out as a taxi, he was afraid to go beyond Plaza San Sebastián. Cochabamba was much bigger than the little town he had come from. He'd gotten lost a lot in the beginning. But bit by bit, the city had revealed itself to him. He now knew most of the streets and knew where everything was in La Cancha, Cochabamba's giant street market. It was good to know things.

"If you're going to keep filling a seat, you'll have to keep filling your belly," the chupe seller said, not so friendly now that she wanted to clear the way for other customers.

Diego slipped off the seat and smiled good-bye. He didn't mind. He understood about customers. He headed back to San Sebastián Square, and into the prison.

"Do you go in and out this much every day?" the new guard asked, annoyed. "Can't you do all your little jobs at once?"

"I'll try," Diego promised. Jobs came as they came. It was better for him if he had a lot to do on one trip instead of going back and forth, but it didn't often work out that way.

Diego walked through the inner prison doors

and into screaming. He stood at the doorway, out of the way of angry women and flying chairs. The guards were sitting back and laughing, waiting for the fighters to calm down. In the men's prison, physical fights were common and dangerous. People had been stabbed, even killed. Arguments in the women's prison lasted longer – for weeks, bitterness would rise and break the surface of the drab daily routine – but they rarely got physical.

Diego tried to figure out why the fight was happening, but it was too far gone. The original quarrel had been forgotten, and now they were angry at everything.

The two most angry women paused to catch their breath, and the guards took advantage of the moment. They hauled the two fighters out of the courtyard and down a hallway to the punishment cells in the basement. Diego had seen the tiny cells once before. He had talked back to a guard, who took him down there and threatened to lock him away if he ever did it again. He didn't know then that children were never put in those cells.

He made a mental note to try to smuggle

Deborah Ellis

some juice or something down to the two women. That would ensure he'd be given their taxi jobs in the future.

The courtyard seemed quiet, now that the fight was over. Diego gave the coca seller the coca leaves and legia, and the piece of paper stating the price. She had some change coming, and they counted it out together.

His mother was pleased with the sweaters, and with the money he'd earned.

"Are you hungry?" she asked him.

"I had a bowl of chupe in the market."

"Good," she said. "I'll just take Corina down for her supper, then, and give you some quiet time."

Every day, Mamá made sure Diego had time to himself in the cell. She said that everyone needed quiet time, especially when they were growing. Usually he did his homework. Sometimes he just stretched out on the bed and let his mind go wherever it wanted.

His own homework was already done, but he picked up some extra money doing homework for some of his classmates, too. He was just finishing this when Mamá and Corina came back.

"There's a football game tonight," Diego said, putting his schoolwork into his book bag and putting the bag up high where Corina couldn't reach it.

"Do you want to go see your papá?" Mamá asked Corina. "You don't mind taking her, do you?"

He liked being asked. "We'll have a run in the park first," he said.

Corina wiggled away from having her face wiped. Mamá handed Diego a shirt of his father's that she had mended. She went down with them to the main door. Corina tried to pull her along with them.

"Mamá, you come, too," she said.

"I can't go with you this time, my precious one," Mamá said. "Diego, go on, take her out."

Diego left quickly. Lingering just made both his mother and Corina cry, even though they'd see each other again in a very short time.

There was still some daylight left, so Diego made monster noises and chased Corina from one corner of the square to the other. They looked for fish in the big pond. He kept her from patting the park dogs. They were too lazy to bite,

Deborah Ellis

but Mamá said they could carry disease and fleas.

Going into the men's prison was the same as going into the women's prison. Two sets of doors, two sets of guards.

The guard on the inside door smiled at Diego and his sister and announced their father's name over the loudspeaker. Diego hoped his father could hear it. There were many more prisoners here than in the women's prison, and most of the men were noisier. The women were usually only noisy when they were arguing.

Corina clung to Diego's leg at the sight of all the loud, big men. He gave her soft hair a bit of a tug so she'd know he knew she was there. Then their father appeared, and she broke away from Diego and into Papá's arms.

Papá cooed over Corina and put his free arm around Diego's shoulders.

"How are you, son?"

"I'm well, Papá." His father was covered in wood dust, and he felt thin as Diego hugged him. "Mamá sent your shirt back."

"Your mamá is well?"

"She is well."

"Does she know how much I miss her? Does she know how much I miss all of you?"

Diego hated it when his father's eyes teared up, and he looked away.

"I sold a doghouse," his father said, changing his tone. "A man who runs a car dealership bought one for his daughter's new pet." He pressed a handful of folded Bolivianos into Diego's hand. The money was covered in sawdust.

"Did you keep some for yourself?" Diego asked, because he knew his mother would want to know. His father shrugged. Diego took some of the money and handed it back to his father. "Have you eaten?" He didn't wait for Papá to answer. He bought a plate of rice and beans from the diner. "We'll go up to the balcony and watch the football game."

Many of the men in the prison had formed football teams. A committee drew up a schedule of matches. This evening, the Narcos were playing the Saints. Diego was going to cheer for the Saints. Juan, one of the players, worked in the prison's jewelry shop, and he sometimes gave Diego taxi jobs.

When his father and sister were settled on the

balcony, Diego went looking for Mando. The men's prison was set up like the women's, only it was bigger. It was officially only two stories high, but overcrowding meant that prisoners had added three more floors of ramshackle cells and makeshift ladders. There was a cell in every possible corner – some too small to stand up in, some with only scraps of cardboard for walls. There were places in the prison, Mando told him, where the guards wouldn't go.

There were women in this prison, too. Some of the men had their wives and children living with them, if they had no place else to go. There were no husbands in the women's prison, though.

Diego checked the woodworking shop on the first floor. Mando sometimes got the job of sweeping up at the end of the day. The machines were quiet now, and the room was empty. Next to it was the shoe shop, smelling strongly of the glue the prisoners used to turn old car tires into sandals and shoes. It was empty, too.

He gave up and went back to his family. Corina was sitting on his father's lap, helping herself to his rice and beans. His father was smiling at her and singing her a little song.

The Saints were in the lead when Mando slid into the seat Diego had saved for him. He was carrying a plastic bag half full of chicha, the corn liquor made in the prison's chichería. He took a long swallow.

"Want some?" he offered Diego.

"No, thanks." He didn't like the taste, and it gave him a headache. Plus, he didn't like the way men behaved when they drank a lot of it. "Does your father mind you drinking it?"

"What's he got to do with it? He's in prison."

Diego changed the subject. "You've missed some good plays. I think the Saints are going to win."

"I've been talking business."

Diego shoved him. "Big tycoon."

"You're absolutely right, big tycoon. You and me both." He looked over at Diego's father and lowered his voice. "Some of the men in here have contacts on the outside. Contacts who can help us make real money."

"Us?"

"You and me." Mando's breath smelled bad from the drink, and Diego had to turn away to inhale. He saw Mando raise the bag of booze in a salute to someone on the other balcony. "Major money."

"There's only one thing that earns major money for people like us, and that's liable to land us right back in here."

"Only if you're not smart. And you and I are smart." Mando's father came up and sat beside his son. "I'll tell you more later," Mando whispered. Diego tried to concentrate on the game and ignore the argument that erupted between the two of them over the chicha.

It was touch and go between the Saints and the Narcos. One of the Narcos hurt himself when he fell on the hard cement courtyard. Diego cheered his team and checked his father now and then to be sure he was eating.

The bare lightbulbs hanging down over the balcony came on – Diego's signal to head back. The game wasn't over, but if he didn't leave now, the doors of the women's prison would be closed for the night. He and Corina could always bunk in with his father – his father didn't have his own cell, but his cellmates would make room for them. He stayed over with his father sometimes. But Corina would miss Mamá and her doll.

"We have to go," he said, standing up. Corina was asleep in Papá's arms. They all went down to the entrance. Papá handed Corina over to Diego.

"Is she too heavy for you?"

"No, I've got her," Diego said. He didn't have to carry her very far.

Their father reached out and cradled their heads in his hands.

"Be well," he said.

Diego went past the guards and out into the street. Whenever he left his father, he felt empty. Whenever he left his mother, he felt empty.

He got back inside the doors of the women's prison just as the guards were preparing to lock up. "One moment longer, and you both would have had to sleep in the park."

Diego thought of the tinkling of the fountains and the coolness of the breeze, the scent of the flowers and the softness of the grass, comparing them with the stuffy cell and the tiny bed.

Then he remembered the street gangs. No place was all good.

CHAPTER FOUR

The morning buzzer was harsh and loud and yanked Diego out of the deep sleep he'd finally sunk into. Corina's restlessness and Mamá's bad dreams had given him a rough night.

The guards banged on the cell walls and doors.

"Everybody up! Down for the count!"

His sister started to cry, as she did every morning. It was more like a whine than a cry, more out of habit than real distress.

"It's the shock of waking up," Mamá had explained to him many times.

"Can't she just get used to it like the rest of us?"

Mamá bundled Corina up in her arms, holding her in her lap while her feet searched the cell floor for her flip-flops.

Diego found his own sandals and pulled on some trousers and a shirt to go over his underwear. Little kids and women could go down to the courtyard in their nightclothes, but he was too old for that.

The children in the prison weren't officially prisoners, but they joined the women in the line-up anyway. The prisoners lined up in the order that they had come to the prison. For awhile, Diego and his family had been at the new end of the line. Now they were about in the middle.

"Presente," each woman yelled out when her name was called. The guards imposed a fine if the reply wasn't loud enough.

Roll call was followed by a rush to the bathrooms. There were always line-ups for the latrines and for the showers. The problem was worse when the water stopped running, as it often did. The reservoir dried up, or there were mechanical problems in the pumping station. Diego read about such things in the newspapers.

The bathrooms stank, too, no matter how much time the prisoners spent cleaning them.

"The stink is in the pipes," his mother said. "Nothing we can do about it. We'll have to get used to it."

He had been there for almost four years, and he wasn't used to it yet.

Diego got himself ready for school while Mamá got Corina ready for daycare. Across the square was a center for children who lived at the prisons. Little kids could go in the morning, and older kids could go after school. Diego sometimes went to play games or do his homework, and to get a free snack of fruit and buns. Mostly, though, he worked as a taxi.

He took his little sister out through the doors and left her with the childcare workers who gathered up children from both prisons before taking them all to the center.

The school Diego went to was fifteen blocks away from the prison. The only uniform they required was a white shirt, which his mother had fresh and clean for him each new school day. He didn't know how she managed it, since there were so few washing sinks and so much competition for them, but his shirt was always ready, along with a clean cloth handkerchief. He used to go to a school that was closer, where other prison kids went, but whenever anything went missing, it was the prison kids who were suspected. Diego was always getting into fights, defending the little ones. One of the workers at the childcare center helped him change schools.

Diego bought a saltena from a sidewalk stand and ate the meat-filled pastry on the way. Although he hurried, he still had to run the last few blocks to make it on time.

"Where is it?" One of his classmates stood outside the school fence, waiting for him. The stocky boy with the expensive running shoes blocked his way at the gate.

"Where's my money?" Diego asked in return.

The classmate gave him five Bolivianos, and Diego handed over his arithmetic homework.

"There are three mistakes in the multiplication, and one of the fraction problems is wrong," Diego told him.

"What? Give me my money back!"

"Don't be an idiot. If you get it all right, she'd know you didn't do it."

The classmate nodded and smiled. "Good thinking. And my composition?"

Diego handed it over. "You wrote about why you like to play football. Better read it over in case she asks you about it. And your spelling is improving — she'll like that."

"It's a little messy."

"I wrote it with my left hand. It looks better than your usual handwriting."

"I oughta pound you."

"Go ahead, but first give me five more Bs for the essay."

The classmate dug into his pocket and gave Diego another crumpled note. "The guy last year only charged me three."

"And last year you almost failed." Diego put the money into his deep pocket and walked away. The classmate was a customer, not a friend. With business concluded, there was nothing more to say.

School was school. Diego kept to himself and did his work. During lunch, he ate the quínoa and beans provided by the school. He propped a book from the school library up in front of his plate and tried not to hear kids complaining about their hardships during the protests.

"Our maid didn't even show up! My mother's going to fire her today."

"We were going to fly to La Paz to see my uncle, but the protesters shut down the airport. It ruined our holiday."

Most of the students at this school were of European descent, and they looked down on people like Diego, but his homework skills were valuable, so they left him alone.

"Can you take Corina with you this afternoon?" Mamá asked him when he got back from school. "I have committee meetings, then chores."

The prison was run by prisoner committees that managed everything from cleaning to settling most disputes. Mamá was on the Welcoming Committee, which helped new prisoners settle in, and the Younger Children's Program Committee, which organized parties for the little ones and tried to get the prison to set aside a space for a playroom. The Works

Committee gave out chores to the other prisoners. This week, Diego's mother had to keep the staircases clean.

"All the guards do is keep us locked in," he'd heard Mamá tell the newcomers. "Everything else is up to us." Except for a serving of bread and milk every morning for prison children, the government provided nothing – not food, not blankets, not even cells. Everybody had to work. Women who couldn't earn money would do chores for women who could.

Corina was straining at her mother's hand. She was in one of those moods when she didn't know what she wanted.

"Yes, I can take her," Diego said. He lifted the box of completed baby clothes off a high shelf. When his mother turned away to put Corina's sandals on, he dropped a length of string into the box as well.

"Don't stay out too late," Mamá said. "There will always be another day."

He liked that she said that, but he knew how much they needed the money.

Corina decided she would like to go out with her brother, and she cooperated with Mamá.

After a trip to the latrine, and with most of the dirt washed off her face, she was ready.

They walked out of the prison. There were no teen gangs around today. Even if there were, they tended not to bother Diego when he was with his sister. They could see she was still a baby. They might jeer him, but from a distance.

He took Corina for a run in the park first, to burn off some of her energy. He made sure they avoided the glue sniffers, a ragged bunch of young men and women heaped together on the grass, passing around a fist-sized plastic pot of glue. They were too dazed from the glue-poison in their brains to be dangerous, but Diego didn't want Corina getting any bad ideas.

Before leaving the square, he bought some toffees from the Aymara woman with the little stand – four toffees for one Boliviano.

"You can have one of these if you're good," he told his sister.

She reached up her little hand for one. "I'm good now."

"As soon as we're settled," he promised.

Diego didn't have a permit to sell things on the street, so he had to watch out for police.

60   *Deborah Ellis*

They could take his money and his goods, and even give him a fine. There was a spot outside the large indoor market on Avenida 25 de Mayo where he'd had luck before, and he headed in that direction.

He found a spot on a clean bit of pavement between a newsstand and someone selling sunglasses. The first thing he did was take the long piece of string out of the box.

"Time for your special bracelet," he said. He tied one end around his sister's ankle. The other end he tied around his own ankle. Corina didn't always sit still the way she was supposed to. This way, if she tried to go anywhere, he'd know.

Corina patiently held out her foot for him. She'd been through this before.

"A special bracelet for a special sister." He got to work setting the baby clothes out on top of the upturned box. He let Corina help, after making sure her hands were clean. Mamá's work was delicate. She turned the old sweaters he found into tiny sleepers, booties and blankets. Diego hoped the people passing by could see how beautiful the work was.

When everything was ready, he gave Corina

one of the candies. She settled down to eat it. Diego stood by the clothes and waited.

Business was slow at first, but it picked up. Diego sold three pairs of booties, a hat and the fanciest of the blankets. Mamá would be pleased.

"Hey, tycoon!" Mando appeared in front of him. "Did you make these doll clothes yourself?"

"Laugh if you want. I made more money in the last hour than you probably made all day." Diego patted his pocket.

Mando had a box of wooden toys with him, made out of scraps from the woodworking shop. The two boys often sold their things together on the street. It was less lonely, and they could watch out for each other. Mando set up his toys on the bottom of his upturned cardboard box, the way Diego set up the baby clothes.

Mando had a quick sale right off the bat – some northern tourist who wanted toys for her children back in the United States. He tucked the Bolivianos away and said, "I'm tired of this – one Boliviano, two Bolivianos. Like I told you, I have a plan to make a lot of money very fast." Mando leaned in close to Diego, although no one on the street was paying attention to them.

Deborah Ellis

"Some of the guys at the prison have friends who are looking to hire boys like us."

"What do you mean, boys like us?"

"Boys who need money. You and me, we could do it together."

"These aren't some kind of creeps, are they? I hear things, you know. Men with big cars hunting for boys."

"No, no, nothing like that. Real work. Honest work."

"There is no honest work that pays a lot of money in a short time, not in Bolivia," Diego said. "There is only smuggling or stealing, and that lands people in jail." He could have added, "Just like your father," but didn't. His fingers felt the Boliviano notes in his pocket. Even though business had been good today, they didn't amount to much. It cost a lot of money to rent a cell, and every month it had to be earned again. "What would we have to do?" he asked, trying not to sound too interested.

"Run errands, I guess. Does it matter? It's money. Plus, we'd get away from here for a few weeks."

"Away?"

"Do you have to talk in questions? It's just a couple of weeks. Then you'll be right back with your mamá, only with a whole lot of money in your pocket."

Diego gave Corina another candy to give himself a moment to think. "I don't see how it would help if I went away," he said. "Aren't you afraid of breaking the law?"

"Laws are made by people with money to keep people like us poor," Mando said. He recited it like it was something he'd learned at school, although Diego didn't think Mando went to school anymore.

"You sound like a protester."

"Nah. They're out for each other. I'm out for myself."

"What does your father say?"

"He'll be glad to be rid of me for awhile."

That told Diego two things. One, that Mando hadn't told his father. Diego had seen Mando and his father together. Even though they argued, his father's face only looked happy when Mando was around. The other was that Mando himself wasn't entirely sure of the whole thing.

Deborah Ellis

He was acting like he was trying to talk himself into something.

"I don't know," Diego said. "Things are hard enough as it is. My parents would worry, and Mamá would have to hire someone else to run errands for her."

"Think about it," Mando said. "I don't leave for a few days, and we'd have fun. I'm tired of earning just a couple of Bolivianos at a time. I'm tired of living at the prison. I'm tired of everything. It will be like a holiday."

"I'll think about it," Diego promised, but there was nothing to think about. Only one type of work paid a lot of money in Bolivia, and that was work connected with cocaine. Diego heard the talk. The women in his mother's prison didn't discuss it much, but the men in his father's prison did. They talked about how much they made, how clever they were, what big plans they had for when they got out. Sometimes fights broke out – someone stabbing someone else over what they did or didn't do on the outside.

Mando grinned and punched Diego on the

arm. "Okay, tycoon, we won't talk any more about it today. Instead, I am going to have all of my toys sold before you even think about selling another piece of your doll clothes."

They shifted into high gear, calling for and hustling customers, and business picked up for the next half hour. An appearance of the police at the other end of the street prompted them to pack up their illegal stands in a hurry and close down shop for the day.

It was time to go home. Diego raised the box of clothes into his arms, took Corina's hand and started to walk.

"Diego, my bracelet!"

He'd forgotten they were still tied together. He untied the string, dropped it in the box, and they were on their way again.

He and Mando – with Corina scampering between them – played football in the park with an old glue bottle. Then it was time to go in.

"Think about it," Mando reminded him. "Unless you expect to get rich some other way."

"I'll be a millionaire before you," Diego said. "And when I am, I certainly won't talk to you anymore. I'll have bodyguards in dark glasses, and a car as long as a bus with dark windows, and you'll bang on the window for centavos, but I will completely ignore you."

"It will be me in that car ignoring you," Mando laughed. "See you tomorrow, tycoon."

Diego watched his friend go into the men's prison. Just before he disappeared through the doors, Mando turned and called out, "Playtime's over, Diego. We're men now." Then he was gone.

Men. Mando was barely fourteen. It was a challenge, though, and Diego knew it. He needed to think.

The evening sun felt good. He sat with Corina on a bench, watching the cars go by, wondering where all the people in the cars were going. Home to supper, probably, to sit in their homes and be with their families, and shut their doors on the rest of the world, like Diego's father once did when he was free and strong. When their work day was behind them, Diego's father would help him with his homework and laugh with Diego's mother about secret jokes between them.

Men. If he were a man, he would not walk back behind the hundred-year-old prison walls.

He would hold out his arm, flag down a passing bus or truck, and go wherever it was going – to a place without guards, without morning counts, and without women crying and screaming.

But what would he do with Corina? Leave her sitting alone on the bench? A man took care of his obligations. He took care of his family.

It would be easy, though. Corina couldn't run very fast. He'd be on the back of a truck and away before she climbed off the bench. It wasn't as though he even liked her all that much. She was whiny and demanding and a whole lot of trouble.

She leaned against him and he realized she'd fallen asleep. He woke her up gently and they went back behind the walls.

The whole prison seemed to be in a bad mood. An argument had broken out among the women in his mother's cooking group. Cooking wasn't allowed in the cells, so several women usually pooled their food and cooked it together. Mice had gotten into a sack of corn and no one wanted to put in money to replace it. Even Diego's mother was yelling.

He finally got his supper, eating with his mother and sister at one of the plastic tables in the courtyard. The only seats available were at the same table with the woman who talked to herself all the time. She kept up a steady stream of one-way conversation while Mamá asked him about school, told him how the committee meetings had gone and tried to look pleased at how much he'd sold. He could tell she was still upset about the argument. A fight broke out between two of the women at the next table, and the guards had to be called in. And while he and his mother were distracted by that, the crazy lady swooped Corina away.

"Call *me* Mamá!" the crazy lady screeched in Corina's face. "Call *me* Mamá!"

"Her own baby died, and she gets confused," Mamá had explained to him once. This wasn't the first time she had gone after Corina.

Two prisoners grabbed Corina and two guards grabbed the crazy woman, managing to pull them apart. A guard hustled the woman down to the punishment cells, and Mamá held Corina tightly.

"You should have been watching her!" she yelled at Diego, then turned her back to him to comfort Corina.

In all the chaos, Diego's supper plate had fallen on the floor. He scooped the food back onto it and ate it anyway. To throw away food would be like tossing Bolivianos into the trash.

It really was an ordinary evening at the prison, but maybe it was Mando talking about going away that made Diego notice these things more. He almost asked Mamá if she remembered their old house, but he stopped himself in time. Of course she remembered. Diego knew she remembered the red flowers that she watered every morning by the front door. She remembered going in and out of that door any time she wanted, without having to depend on an unreliable angel to open it. She remembered having her own kitchen where she could go in the middle of the night for a snack, or just because she felt like wandering. Corina didn't remember any of those things because she'd been born in the prison, but Mamá remembered, and so did Papá, and so did Diego.

His parents had to stay in jail thirteen more

years. As he sat at the table, the remains of his dinner in front of him, Diego wrote the number thirteen in nice, tidy numbers in a notebook in his mind. Then he added twelve, his age now, and drew a line under the sum. He added them both together, and stared at the total in his mind for a long, long time.

CHAPTER FIVE

"Can you watch Corina for awhile?" Mamá asked the next evening. "I need a break."

The three of them were in the cell. Diego was stretched out on the bed.

"I have homework," he said.

"There's no school tomorrow. You can do your homework later."

"I don't want Diego to watch me," Corina whined.

"Please, Diego. It's been a long day. I won't be long. I'll just go downstairs and have some juice and play some cards."

"I want juice!" Corina demanded.

"All right, all right, I'll watch her." It was the last thing Diego wanted to do, but if he said no, his mother would sit in the cell and make him feel guilty.

Mamá didn't wait around for him to change his mind, or for Corina to complain some more. She lifted Corina onto the bed where she couldn't get down easily and left the cell.

Corina whined and started hitting Diego.

"Quit it!"

But she wouldn't. Diego ignored her as long as he could, tried to push her away, and finally gave up. She'd be less annoying if he entertained her.

"Want me to draw some pictures for you?"

"No."

"Tell me what you want, and I'll draw it."

"Cat."

Diego drew a cat, then all the other animals Corina knew, then a tree, a bird, a car. Then she wanted to draw her own pictures, so he put her on the floor with a paper and pencil. She chattered for a bit, but finally fell quiet, so Diego was able to concentrate on his own work again.

His own homework was done, and now he was working on a math assignment for someone two grades ahead of him. It was more complicated than the work he usually did in class. He had to concentrate hard to figure it out, but he was enjoying himself. The math was a puzzle, a mystery, and he was unraveling it. It took awhile, but at last it was done.

"Okay, Corina, now we can play," he said, tucking the arithmetic into his book bag.

There was no reply. Diego looked down from the bed to the spot on the floor where Corina had been sitting. The paper and pencil were there, but Corina wasn't.

She was probably under the bed, expecting him to crawl under there and drag her out. Let her stay.

He opened his book bag and got out a small rubber ball he'd found that day in the street. He turned it around in his hands. One of the sides was a little chewed up, and it looked like there were teeth marks on it. Some dog was missing its toy.

He wished they allowed pets in the prison. If he had a dog instead of a little sister, it could sleep on a blanket by the bed, and he could reach down during the night and it would lick his hand. He could take it out with him on taxi runs, and throw the ball for it in the park. He'd keep it away from the park dogs, so it wouldn't catch their diseases, and it would keep the gangs from bothering him.

Diego tossed the ball up in the air and bounced it against the wall.

"You're being awfully quiet, Corina," he said. "Too bad you can't be like this all the time."

There was no answer. She was probably asleep. Diego was tempted to leave her there, but Mamá would not be pleased if she came back and saw that he hadn't done his job properly. Mamá didn't think the floor was clean enough for Corina to sleep on, no matter how many times she washed it down.

Diego pounded on the wall. "Hey, Corina, wake up!"

There was no reply. Diego sighed and swung his legs over the edge of the bed.

"You are so much trouble," he said. "Why can't you grow up?"

He stood up, then crouched down to peer under the bed. He saw boxes and bags storing their belongings, but no Corina.

Children – especially little children – were not allowed to wander around the prison on their own. It was the most important rule. Some of the prisoners were crazy, like the one who went after Corina. Others didn't like children. It was even more serious in the men's prison, where some of the men were violent, especially to children, and there were tools and machines that children could break or be hurt by.

Parents who didn't supervise their children weren't allowed to keep them in the prison. Government people would come and take the children away.

Diego's panic grew. He wanted to run out into the hall and scream Corina's name, but he couldn't, because then everybody would know she was missing. He made himself pause for a moment and leave the room slowly. He hoped he looked normal, and that no one could hear his heart pounding.

There was no sign of Corina in the hallway. Diego popped his head into the cells near his mother's on his way to the balcony. Corina was small. She could be anywhere.

If she was bored, she'd probably go looking for Mamá. She'd wanted some juice. If she found her way safely down the stairs to their mother,

Mamá would be angry at Diego for not watching her more closely, but nothing worse than that would happen.

Diego couldn't see his sister on the balcony. He peered over the railing. Mamá was below, at one of the tables in the courtyard, drinking juice and talking with her friends. Corina was not there. He leaned over to try to see more of the courtyard. Directly below him was a woman cooking a pot of chupe, but no Corina.

He leaned over a little farther. Maybe Corina was with one of the prisoners who ran a little shop. Corina was always begging for candy.

He hadn't even realized he was still holding the ball. Somehow, it slipped from his hand. It fell right into the pot. The soup splattered up, the woman jumped, lost her balance, and knocked the whole pot over onto the cement floor.

And Diego lost all hope of being able to get through this crisis with nobody knowing.

Mamá understood immediately. She was up the stairs and standing beside Diego before he'd gotten over the shock of dropping the ball. She gave him one look, then checked their cell.

"Where have you looked?" she asked when she came out.

"I just started," he said. "She can't be far."

Mamá went one way, he went another.

The prison was a small world. News traveled almost instantly. The good part was that everyone joined in the search. The bad part was that everyone knew Diego hadn't done his job, and that meant Mamá hadn't done her job. Mamá's friends were sympathetic and kind. The women who weren't so nice said Mamá was a bad parent and Diego was too stupid to ever be hired as a taxi again.

Diego heard it all as he moved through the prison, looking high and low for his missing little sister.

"I always thought you were a good kid," Guard López told him, as he searched under the shelves near the prison doors. "I guess I was wrong. I guess you're in the right place after all."

Nothing anyone said could make Diego feel worse than he already did.

"She didn't go outside, did she?" he asked Guard López.

Guard López was in the middle of saying she wasn't a babysitter when Diego heard a shout.

"I found her!"

The call sounded across the courtyard. An inmate ran out of a hallway on the main floor, holding a crying Corina. Mamá took her and went upstairs.

No one said anything to Diego. He sat by himself at one of the plastic tables until the lights-out buzzer sounded.

As he passed the woman whose food he had ruined, he heard her say, "I'll let your mother know how much she owes me for the soup."

Diego didn't reply. Slowly, he climbed the stairs, and because he didn't want to get his mother into any more trouble, he went into their cell and went to bed.

She kept her back to him all night long, and didn't speak.

The Prisoners' Disciplinary Committee didn't waste any time. They met the very next day. When they had finished talking, they called for Diego and his family to appear.

The committee met in the room that served as a chapel on Sundays and as an adult education room at other times. A large cross hung over one end, and there were tables and chairs that could be moved around.

Diego had never been summoned to meet the committee before. The other times Mamá had been fined because he'd been running on the stairs or talking back to a guard, she had gone alone to hear what the fine would be. Sometimes it was money, sometimes it was extra chores.

The committee sat at a long table, under the cross. There was a single chair in front of the table where Mamá sat with Corina. Diego stood beside his mother.

The head of the committee spoke. "Being in prison is not what any of us would want. By governing ourselves, we try to make this horrible place a little more livable. This committee was elected by the inmates to keep order and settle disputes. Not for the sake of the guards or the administration, but for the sake of each other."

Just get on with it, Diego thought.

They did. Their first ruling was one he expected.

"You will have to pay for the pot of soup that was ruined. We are charging you to pay what

Mrs. Verde would have earned if she had sold the whole pot." There was a price per bowl, times the number of bowls in the pot. It came to a lot of Bolivianos. Diego would have to double his number of taxi runs and take on more homework. Even then, it would take him weeks.

"We have no power to rule on whether your children should remain at the prison or not. That is up to the prison administration and the Department of Child Welfare."

Mamá stiffened and grabbed Diego tightly around the waist. He knew her grip on Corina was tight, too.

The committee woman continued. "Being able to keep our children with us is the only thing that gets us through this. Prison is not a place for children, but it is better that they be here with us instead of in some government home or on the streets. Our rules of supervision are so strict because the world is so short of compassion.

"However, this is the first time in the four years you have been here that anything like this has happened. We recognize your contributions to our little community, both yours and your son's. We will recommend to the administration that your children be allowed to stay with you."

Diego could feel his mother sobbing with relief. He put his arm around her shoulder.

"Diego," the committee head began. Diego's head snapped up. "You are no longer a small child. Your inattention to your responsibility could have ended in disaster. Your sister could have been hurt, and that would have meant that none of us could keep our children here. It is wrong to have to carry such responsibility at your age, but the world is the way it is. You caused an uproar in the whole prison. If you cannot be trusted to look after your little sister, you cannot be trusted to run errands. Therefore, until further notice, you will not be able to work as a taxi."

Diego could feel the eyes of every prisoner on him as he left the meeting room with his family. Shame mixed with rage. How could they take away his livelihood? How was he supposed to pay back for what he did if he couldn't earn money? Sure, he had been wrong, but this was not justice!

He knew what it would be like, how his

mother would have to hand over all the money she'd gotten from his father, and all the money she earned from knitting, just to pay for the spoiled soup.

How would she be able to keep paying rent for a cell? They would have to go back to living on a mat in the courtyard. Corina would become even harder to manage, and Diego's private time would disappear.

If he was no longer a taxi, he'd have no reason to leave the prison except for school. He'd spend endless hours and days stuck behind the high stone walls, looking after his sister, in the shadow of his mother's disapproving silence.

CHAPTER SIX

Mando was waiting for Diego when school got out the next day.

"Bad luck," he said.

"How did you know?" Diego asked. Then he remembered he wasn't the only kid in the women's prison with a father in the men's.

"Are you going to stay with your father for awhile? You could stay in my father's cell with me if there's no room in your father's."

"I thought about it, but that would only make things worse. The committee lets me run errands for my mother, but if I'm not there, she'll have to pay a taxi. And if I look after Corina, she can get more knitting done."

"How deep are you in the hole?"

Diego told him. Mando whistled.

"I know a way out of the hole," Mando said. "You could solve your problem and even come out way ahead."

"My mother would be furious."

"Could she be any angrier with you than she is now?"

Diego thought it was possible, but he wasn't sure. His mother wasn't yelling at him, but there was an awful lot of silence pointed in his direction. It was worse than yelling. It was like she was trying to pretend that he wasn't there.

"We're leaving tomorrow," Mando said.

Diego didn't say anything for awhile, then, "How much money would we make?"

"I don't know for sure, but probably more than we'd make in a year of taxi jobs."

"And we'll be gone only two weeks?"

"Give or take a day or two. We'll be back before you've even realized you've left."

Diego calculated in his head. He'd tell his mother he was going to stay with his father. A note would be better.

"We won't be smuggling, will we?" he asked. "People get caught when they smuggle." This time he had to add, to drive home the point, "Your father got caught."

"My father was stupid," Mando said. "But, no, little boy, it's not smuggling, just running errands for the big bosses. You think they'd trust something so valuable to a couple of kids they don't know?"

Running errands didn't sound so bad. That was what he did now.

"What will we tell our parents?"

"Our parents are in prison," Mando said. "They can't even tell themselves what to do. We have to decide for ourselves." He stopped walking. "Look, it's very simple. You're coming or you're not. Once you decide that, the rest can get figured out. Only…I hope you come. I really don't want to go alone."

"Will they have a job for me?"

"Waiting and ready, with your name on it – Reserved for Tycoon Diego. I already told them you were coming. So, you see? You have to."

Diego grinned. A decision had been made. He felt better already.

They made arrangements to meet up the next

morning. Mando had other jobs to do, so he had to run.

"Bring some money," he said as he headed away. "Just to have in your pocket, you know, for snacks and things. You'll look like a hick if you arrive with nothing."

"If I had money to bring, I wouldn't need to go with you," Diego muttered.

"If it's money you want, help me move these flour sacks," a shopkeeper who had heard him said. "My regular helper is late, and this truck needs to be unloaded and moved before the traffic police give me a ticket."

Diego jumped at the chance. For the next two hours, he moved sacks from the back of the truck to the back of the shop. The sacks were nearly as big as he was and almost as heavy. He had to be taught how to carry them.

"Back yourself up to the truck, grab two corners of a bag, and let it fall onto your back."

Diego was nearly doubled over by the weight of the bag, and when the job was done, he was aching all over and covered with flour. But the shop owner was pleased, gave him fifteen Bolivianos and asked him to keep in touch.

"I may have to fire my helper, even if he is my brother-in-law," he said.

Cochabamba was starting to get dark. Diego headed back to the prison as quickly as he could. Each step was painful, and he was bone-weary. He made it back just in time.

"You again," the new guard said. "One day we'll lock up early, and you'll be out of luck, won't you?"

For two whole weeks, I won't have to see your ugly face, Diego thought. He began to look forward to leaving.

Mamá didn't ask where he'd been, and he didn't tell her. She didn't even look up from her knitting. He didn't see Corina. Mamá must have arranged babysitting with one of the other mothers — you watch my child for two hours today, I'll watch yours for two hours tomorrow.

"I'm going to take a shower," he said, just to say something. He found some clean clothes and went down to the washroom. The cold water came out in a trickle, but it was enough.

The cell was empty when he got back. Mamá

was giving him his nightly private time. There was no point in doing his homework. Diego put his flour-covered clothes in his book bag, added a few other things he might need, and put the bag up on the shelf. He wrote his mother a note, saying he would be staying with his father for two weeks. He'd slip it under a pillow just before leaving in the morning.

Getting to sleep was impossible. Diego's mind would not shut down. Sharing a bed makes the night very long if you can't sleep. Diego couldn't move without waking someone up. Minutes trickled by. The morning buzzer was a relief.

Last count for two weeks, Diego thought, as he stood in line with the prisoners and their children. The next morning he would wake up a free man, doing a free man's labor for a free man's wages. As the guards went down the row of women, calling out names and checking faces, Diego couldn't even imagine what that would be like.

The morning rush was the same as the morning rush always was. Diego hid the note, then waited in the courtyard with his mother and his little sister for the guards to open the doors to let the children out. He tightened his grip around his book bag full of clothes and felt in his pocket for the few Bolivianos he was taking with him. They were there, safe beside his handkerchief.

He wanted to say something special to Mamá, to tell her not to worry about him, that things were going to turn out all right. But he didn't have the right words. He wanted her to reach out and hug him, to read his mind and tell him not to go, that she wasn't angry and had found a way to fix things, that he wasn't a disappointment to her. But he guessed she couldn't find the words, either.

In the next instant, he was through the doors and outside the prison.

Diego headed off in the direction of his school, in case his mother had developed x-ray eyes and could see through the prison walls. Then he turned down some side streets, broke into a run, and kept running until he got to the Plaza Colón.

The plaza hummed with small businesses selling candy from cardboard boxes, biscuits from wooden stalls on wheels, and saltenas from portable ovens. Men in suits and women in business dresses hurried to their office jobs, tourists peered at maps and squinted at street signs, beggars staked out their morning territory.

At first, Diego couldn't see Mando among all the trees and activity. Then he spotted his friend right in the center of the square by the big fountain. He waved and headed over.

"Now what?" Diego asked.

"They'll be along."

"Who?"

"The men who hired us."

"Do you know where we're going?"

"Money Mountain," Mando said. "You're such a worrier. You're an old man already."

"I just want everything to go well. It doesn't hurt to be careful."

"You have to live a little," Mando said. "You can be too careful."

"You can also end up like them." Diego nodded toward three boys lying on the grass near the fountain. He could smell them from across the pathway as they passed a plastic glue pot around, breathing deeply.

Mando shrugged.

Diego hopped on and off the side of the fountain,

too nervous to sit still. He almost hoped the men wouldn't show.

"Afraid your mamá is going to come out here and stop you?" Mando teased.

"Sure," Diego said, grinning, "but not as afraid as you are of your father finding out."

After that, they both relaxed a little, and a moment later, two men were standing in front of them.

Mando leapt to his feet. "This is Paolo," he said, nodding at the slimmer of the two men. "His brother works in the prison shoe shop. And this is Rock."

"This is your friend?" Rock asked Mando, without even saying hello.

Diego stood up and held out his hand. "I'm Diego. Thank you for giving me a job."

"He's too small," Paolo said, ignoring his outstretched hand.

"I am not!" Diego exclaimed, not knowing what he was not too small to do.

"He's small but he's very strong," Mando said. "He can beat me up."

"My little sister could beat you up," Rock said. "All right, it's your funeral. If we're not happy with you, we'll feed you to the alligators. Where are the others?"

"What others?" Mando asked.

"I talked to three other boys from one of the other prisons. Let's not wait. Hey, you!" He called out to the three glue sniffers. They looked up with unfocussed eyes. "Come along, you'll make some money."

It took the boys a long time to get the message from their brains to their feet.

"We can do better than that," Paolo said.

"We don't need better," Rock said. "Let's go, boys. Small boy, bring the others along."

The two men turned and walked away quickly, Mando keeping up. Diego tried not to breathe in the stink of the street boys as he hustled them along the path after the others. He wasn't sure they had really agreed to come, but they looked like they could use some money, and whatever they were heading into was certainly better than what they were doing now.

"It's your lucky day," he told them.

"Want some?" One of the boys offered him the glue pot. He shook his head and pushed them along.

On a small street several blocks from the square, the men stopped in front of a high steel gate. One of them unlocked the padlock, unwound the chain and opened one side of the gate to a parking lot. Diego opened the other side, securing it with a hook. He'd make himself so useful, they soon wouldn't notice his size.

"In the back," the man said, jerking his head at a pick-up truck. Mando and the other boys climbed in. Mando held out his hand to help Diego, but Diego shook his head.

"I'll lock the gate up after we go through," he said.

The truck moved slowly out onto the narrow street. Diego secured the gate, snapped the padlock shut and hopped into the back with the others. He knocked on the roof of the cab a couple of times to signal that he was in and the truck could now move.

"Big tycoon," Mando said, grinning. Diego grinned back.

He looked around for his book bag with his spare clothes, and remembered he'd left it leaning against the fountain wall in the square.

"I forgot my bag!" he told Mando.

"So what? With the money we make, you'll be able to buy a dozen new ones."

Diego liked that thought – a new bag, new clothes, new everything, his debts paid off and money to spare.

Oh, it felt fine to be riding like kings through the city, sun beaming down, adventure ahead. The boys knocked against the truck and each other as it turned this way and that through the streets of Cochabamba. The truck even drove within two blocks of the prison. Diego felt his chest expanding. It was wonderful to be alive, wonderful to be heading off to do a good thing, wonderful to spend the next two weeks without guards or line-ups or smelly toilets, or the clicking of knitting needles, or his mother's angry, disappointed silence.

They climbed up into the hills behind the city, up past clusters of tiny shacks, up higher even than the giant white statue of Christ whose outstretched arms blessed the city. Diego could see that Cochabamba was at the bottom of a bowl made by the hills around it. He'd been brought into the bowl in a dark police truck, and hadn't been out of it since his parents were arrested.

Suddenly, he felt a little scared. His parents were getting farther and farther away with each roll of the truck wheels.

"I'll be back in two weeks," he whispered into the noise of the engine.

Then Mando tossed a toffee at him. They chewed candy and watched the scenery, and Diego felt fine again.

A few hours out, when the sun was straight above them, they stopped at a roadside eatery run out of the front of a small house. Plates of lamb stew appeared, along with chicha and soda. Diego wondered if the money in his pocket would be enough, but one of the men paid for everybody. He felt better about the whole trip, seeing how well they'd be taken care of. Mando and Diego and the other three boys shoveled in the stew and guzzled the chicha, although Diego opted for an orange soda instead.

The men wanted to take a little rest after lunch, and they stretched out in the shade. Mando and the other boys slept, too, but Diego was afraid of not waking up when the men did, and being left behind. The family who ran the eatery had several small children. Diego played with the kids and talked with their mother while the others slept. It was like being back in his old life, for a short while.

Back on the road, the scenery started to change as the red rocks and dirt began to be replaced with patches of grass and scrub trees. Diego tried to keep his eyes open, but his sleepless night, the hot sun, and the rhythm of the road put him quickly to sleep.

He woke up when the truck stopped again. Gone were the yellow rocky hills of the Altiplano. They had been replaced by greens and trees and smoky air, and Diego realized he was in a whole other world.

CHAPTER SEVEN

"It's empty."

A grimy, empty plastic glue pot was pushed under Diego's nose by one of the equally grimy glue boys.

"That's not good for you, you know," Diego told him. "It destroys your brain. We learned about it in school."

"It's empty," the boy said again. He looked so sad, his bloodshot eyes begging Diego to fix the problem. The other two boys bumped into him the way Diego had seen baby goats bump into each other at feeding time.

"What's your name?" Diego asked.

That was one question the boy could answer. "Roberto. This is my brother, Julio." Julio was the smaller of the two. Maybe there was a family resemblance under all that dirt. The other boy, a long, thin lad, wavered a bit, then turned and puked over the side of the truck.

"That's Domingo," Roberto said, thrusting the glue pot forward again. "It's empty."

"Somebody is going to have to clean my truck, and it had better be you, small boy, so eager to prove yourself," Paolo called out to Diego over his shoulder, slamming the truck door shut.

Diego climbed down from the truck on legs made wobbly by the long journey. He turned to Mando for any ideas about how to clean Domingo's puke off the side of the truck, but Mando was too busy trying to look tough and confident, the way Diego had seen him act sometimes in the prison.

Diego briefly considered leaving it for Domingo — after all, he put it there — but Domingo and the other glue boys were stumbling and looking very lost. Besides, Diego was a taxi. He was in the business of getting jobs done.

Rock and Paolo were talking to other men in the village, ignoring the boys. Diego moved his legs around to get some circulation back into them, and took a look at where they had ended up.

All he could see was green. Even the sky had a green haze to it. They were in a small valley, surrounded by green hills. The road they had come in on was a dirt track, so full of holes that Diego wondered how he could possibly have slept while driving over them.

He noticed some houses set among the hills, but they were different from any houses he had ever seen. For one thing, they were mounted on poles, not sitting on the ground. For another, the houses were made of branches, leaves and thatch, not stone and cement like the houses in Cochabamba and his old village. Women and girls tended cookfires in the yards. Old men and children sat at tables underneath the platforms of the houses. They looked at Diego with no interest.

Still, he had a job to do. He walked up to one of them, picked up a plastic bucket from the ground near the cookfire, and tried a few words in Spanish. There was no response, and he didn't know enough Aymara to ask to borrow the pail, so he acted out barfing and cleaning it up. They

100   *Deborah Ellis*

laughed and pointed to a stagnant pond at the edge of the trees. Diego splashed water on the truck and returned the bucket. It felt good to make the strangers laugh, and to get the task done.

He rejoined Mando, who was sitting with the other boys in the shade of a tree.

"What do we do now?"

"How would I know?" Mando replied.

The heat of the little village was heavier than the heat in Cochabamba. Diego was suddenly very thirsty. He headed over to the little tienda. The other boys followed him.

He greeted the woman minding the little shop.

"*K'guaka?*" he asked, pointing to bottles of orange soda cooling in a pail of water, and using the little bit of Aymara he'd learned at the prison.

"*Paya,*" the woman said. Two Bolivianos.

Diego looked back at the boys behind him. He guessed from the state of their clothes that they didn't have any money.

"*Quimsa,*" he said, holding up three fingers and handing over six Bolivianos. "We'll share," he said to Mando.

"Thanks, tycoon," Mando said, taking the first drink. Diego passed the two other bottles to the other three boys. That still left him with a bit of money.

They took their sodas back to the shade and sat down, passing the bottles back and forth.

Diego kept glancing at Mando. Mando was older, and he should really be taking charge, but he wasn't. He kept slapping at insects and looking up at the hills.

Maybe they did things differently at the men's prison, but Diego had sat through enough of his mother's committee meetings at the women's prison to know what was important.

"We're all new to this," he said. "We don't know each other, but if we all watch out for each other…"

He let his voice trail away. The glue boys had too much fog in their heads to be part of a discussion, and Mando was too busy pretending not to be nervous.

Diego decided not to worry. Sure, the other boys were bigger, but they didn't seem like bullies. Even if they were, he'd seen his parents deal with bullies in prison. "Don't try to be stronger, and don't let them think you're weaker," his papá told him. "Be proud to be yourself. Bullies don't know how to deal with people like that, and they will leave you alone." Diego was pretty sure he could handle anything these guys might dish out to him, if their brains ever cleared up enough for them to make trouble.

"Did we bring you all the way out here to sit on your backsides, or are you going to work?" one of the men shouted at them.

The boys all got to their feet – Diego and Mando jumping up, the others rising in a sort of stagger – and headed over to the truck where the men were standing. Diego gathered up the empty bottles and ran them over to the woman in the shop.

"I see we have a little gentleman with us," Rock said. "You're not too refined to do a little work, are you?"

Diego grinned and showed his muscles. It wasn't that funny, but everyone laughed, even the men.

"Three hours of daylight left. Let's not waste them," Paolo said. Everybody got back into the truck. Diego stood up, clinging to the roof. He wanted to see where they were going, not just where they had been.

The road they turned down didn't even look like a road, but what did that matter? Diego was with his friend, and the sheer joy of movement made him laugh and laugh, even when leaves hanging down across the road slapped him in the face.

The truck came to a stop moments later, at a clearing where local coca farmers had spread their coca leaves out on big sheets to dry in the sun.

"It's like coming home," Diego said, grabbing Mando's arm. "My parents did that! I used to help them."

He remembered the way they would talk while they worked, imagining what to buy with the sale of their crop – shoes and school books, warm blankets, a few more chickens. Diego would help his mother spread the leaves, and his father would do the heavier work of bundling them for the market.

Now Diego was doing the heavy work. He threw himself into it. Mando tried to keep up, fumbled a lot. The glue boys were hopeless.

Rock had to keep screaming to get them to do anything.

"Faster, faster!" the men kept yelling. "The sun's going down!"

Diego and the others worked faster, tying the leaves into bundles, tossing the bundles onto the truck. The pile of bundles got higher and higher. Rock told Domingo and Julio to climb up onto the bundles, and the other boys tossed the sacks of leaves up to them.

"Here is your payment." Diego's eyes grew as wide as supper plates as Rock took a large roll of Bolivianos out of his pocket, peeled off a chunk of notes and handed them to the cocalero.

He was putting the money back in his pocket when he saw Diego staring.

"You want this money?" he asked, coming closer, holding out the wad of bills. He pushed the money right into Diego's face.

Nobody else moved. Even the birds seemed to stop singing.

"Go ahead, tough guy, try and grab it. Or maybe you think you'll try to steal it from me in the middle of the night?"

"I was just admiring your success," Diego

said, as calmly as he could. He looked straight at the man's face. To look away would show he was afraid. Never show bullies you are afraid.

Rock slapped Diego on the nose with the wad of money.

"Smart boy," he said. "We don't need smart boys. We need stupid boys with strong backs and strong legs." He put the money back in his pocket. "My name is Rock," he said, "because I will land on your head like a rock if you try to cross me. Let's go!" he yelled.

"Rock?" Mando whispered to Diego. "More like pebbles." Jokes about manhood were common in the men's prison.

They got back to the clearing where they had started out. The sun was going down behind the hills. The noise of the jungle insects was deafening. Diego wasn't used to such darkness. At night in prison, lights in the courtyard and hallways were always on. The only time it got really dark was when there was a power failure.

The only light in the little valley came from the cookfires and kerosene lanterns hung from the stilt-houses. Diego's body ached from the hard work, and the long day. He was looking forward to sleeping.

"Where are we spending the night?" he asked.

"In the jungle, smart boy," Rock said. "Everybody grab a sack."

"In the jungle?" Diego didn't understand.

"Let's just do what they tell us," Mando said. "They have the money."

It made no sense, but Diego complied. He knew from moving flour bags how to carry a sack. He backed up to the truck, grabbed the sack and moved away. The bundle of coca leaves slapped him on the back. It was big, but not heavy, not compared to the flour. The other boys followed his example.

"That will get you started," Rock said. He nodded his head toward the forest. "All right, don't stand around like a bunch of goats. Smart boy, you go first. You can scare away the snakes."

A path led up through the grass beside the stilt houses. It led to the edge of the forest.

"Into the bush," Rock said, bringing up the rear with a couple of other men.

"What? Where?"

"There's a path. Move it. We've got work to do."

Diego didn't move. He still didn't see any path.

"You want our money, smart boy? You're going to have to earn it." Rock pulled away a low hanging branch. There was just enough moonlight for Diego to see a bit of a pathway. "In," he ordered.

Snakes, thought Diego, and plunged ahead.

CHAPTER EIGHT

For the next two hours, Diego walked almost blindly through the jungle. The nightmarish screams of monkeys and the calls of tree frogs came at him from the dark.

He had never been in the jungle before. He'd lived with his family high in the hills and then he was a prison kid, a city kid. His nights were bare lightbulbs burning, women and children crying, guards yelling and keys clanging. He hated it, but it was what he was used to.

He almost wished he were back there.

"Mando, are you there?"

"Right behind you, tycoon."

"Did you know about this?"

"No, but it all leads to money. Is it too hard for you?"

"I'm just worried about you." Diego adjusted his grip on his sack of coca leaves. "I'd hate to have to tell your father that you'd been eaten by, well, whatever there is out here to eat you."

"You won't have to tell my father anything, tycoon. It will be me bringing what's left of your body back to your mother in a little bundle."

"Still alive up there, smart boy?" Rock called from the back of the line.

"I'm alive, but I don't know where I'm going," he called back.

"Just follow the path."

"How do I know if it's the right path?" Diego asked. "I think I saw another path branch off this one. Are you sure you want me to lead?"

"What? Hold it. Everybody stop." Diego heard Rock coming up through the line of boys and bundles. "You saw another trail?"

"I think so," Diego said. "It's hard to tell. Why can't we have flashlights?"

"Why do you think, smart boy?"

Because you're too stupid to carry one, Diego thought, but he knew the real reason. They didn't want to be spotted by the soldiers who patrolled Bolivia looking for drug producers and smugglers.

The air of the jungle was hot and heavy, but Diego felt a chill run through his body.

"No, this is the right way," Rock said. "It has to be. I've been on this trail many times during the day. Guess you're not so smart after all, are you, smart boy?"

"I guess not."

Rock started walking. Diego and the others kept up behind him.

Now who's scaring away the snakes, Diego thought.

Behind him, the glue boy at the back started to whimper. The men at the rear told him to shut up, and gave him such a hard shove that all the other boys were shoved, too.

The bag of leaves started to feel heavier, and it was awkward to carry. Diego's shoulders began to cramp. The bottle of soda he'd shared with Mando was a million years ago.

Worst of all were the bugs. With his hands busy hanging on to the coca, he couldn't brush or wave away the bugs from his face. Mosquitoes

I Am a Taxi   111

bit his flesh and buzzed around his ears, and tiny bugs flew into his eyes, making them tear up.

Just when Diego had begun to give up hope that they would ever arrive anywhere, the jungle trail opened up to a small clearing. Several men were already there, sitting at a table under a dark tarp slung from tree branches. A few lanterns hung under the awning and gave the clearing a bit of light.

"Home sweet home," Rock announced.

The boys dropped their sacks of coca leaves and made circles with their arms and shoulders. Diego wanted to drop to the ground and sleep, snakes or no snakes.

"We need a pit dug," Rock said.

"Can we rest first?" Diego asked. "Just for a little while?"

"You can dig or you can turn around and walk back to Cochabamba, prison boy."

Diego wondered when he had gone from smart boy to prison boy.

"Something to drink?" Mando asked. "We'll work better after a drink of water."

One of the men jerked his thumb in the direction of the far end of the sheltered area. Mando found the covered barrel first. A cup hung from it. The boys took turns drinking. The water made Diego feel better.

"Are you okay?" he asked Roberto, who seemed more baffled than the rest of them to find himself in the middle of the jungle.

"Why are we here?" Roberto asked. "I don't want to be here."

"Maybe we should ask for food," Diego suggested.

"Let's not push our luck," Mando said.

"It's not pushing our luck to ask for food when we're hungry," Diego started to say, but he was interrupted by Rock.

"Smart boy! Put everybody to work or we'll feed you to the anacondas!"

"Anacondas?" Mando whispered.

"Big snakes," Diego replied. He led the others away from the water barrel.

Two of the men put up another tarp over an empty section of the clearing. Another small lantern was lit.

"Start digging," Rock said, passing out shovels. The men argued about how big the trench should be. When they reached an agreement, they marked an outline on the ground, and the boys started to dig.

The earth was soft from all the jungle debris, but the digging would have gone faster if the boys were not so tired.

"Take your time," Rock sneered. "We don't care if you sleep or not."

"Some crop of babies you brought this time," one of the other men said.

"The dregs of the dregs," Rock said. "They'll work cheap and keep their mouths shut. Except for this one." Rock tossed a handful of dirt at Diego's head. Diego flinched, but kept digging. "This one's got an attitude."

"That won't do him much good out here, will it?"

Diego kept digging.

The pit they dug was ten feet long, four feet wide, and two feet deep. Diego used the notebook in his head to figure out the cubic area. It helped to pass the time.

The boys got to sit down for a few minutes after that. Julio fell asleep against Diego's shoulder. He had no more weight than a sheaf of grass. Diego stayed awake and watched the men put a big plastic tarp into the pit, supporting it on all sides so that the tarp lined the pit and rose two feet above the ground level.

"Smart boy – you and your friend start dumping those leaves in here."

Diego carefully shifted so Julio could slide to the ground without waking up. He got to his feet.

"My name is Diego," he said.

"You don't want me to know your name," Rock said. "Once something goes in here," he tapped his head, "it never goes away."

Diego doubted that, but he and Mando got to work. Diego had no idea what they were doing, but, like Mando said, it would all end up with money, and that was all that mattered. They undid the ties on the sacks of coca leaves and emptied them into the newly dug pit.

The men started arguing again. "It's two cans of kerosene to three sacks of leaves."

"No, you're wrong. That's not how we did it before, and we have five sacks of leaves tonight, not three."

"Did you use the big cans, or those other cans? And how much water and sulphuric acid?"

"Maybe we should wait for Smith. We don't want to waste the leaves."

"We're not waiting for Smith. He expects to find this pit up and running," Rock said. "Oh, this is just wonderful. We have everything here, but nobody knows the proportions."

"Proportions are ratios," Diego said, his mouth talking before his mind told him to keep quiet.

"What's that, smart boy? You trying to tell us our business?"

Mando put his hand on Diego's arm to shut him up, but Diego kept going. "Ratios are fractions, and I'm good at fractions."

"You think you're smarter than me?"

"Maybe you had better things to do the day they covered fractions at school."

Rock crossed the clearing in two steps and struck Diego across the face.

The blow hurt, but it didn't surprise him. Diego stood his ground. Never show bullies that you are afraid.

"That's enough," one of the men said. "We have work to do. Kid, come over here. What can you make of this?"

He held a crumpled piece of paper under a flashlight. Diego could see words and numbers scratched on it in a mess. It looked like some kid's cheat sheet at school.

He looked at it for a long minute, and it began to make sense.

"Do you have paper and pen?" he asked.

"Oh, yes, right next to our computer," Rock snarled.

Another man took a small notebook and a pen out of his pocket and handed them to Diego.

It's a puzzle, Diego thought. He connected the pen to his mind and got to work.

"This is what you need," he said, handing the notebook back with the completed sum.

"Let me see!" Rock grabbed the paper, frowned at it like he was redoing the calculations in his head and said, "Yes, this looks right."

The other boys, wide awake again, giggled, but Diego kept a straight face. Stupid people could be dangerous.

"Could we have something to eat?" he asked politely. "The lamb stew you bought us was great, but it was a long time ago."

"We'll give you something better than food," the

man said. "You'd better appreciate this. You'd never be able to afford it in your regular lousy lives."

The boys crowded around while he rolled them cigarettes with loose tobacco and a gumlike substance mixed together. Even Mando was excited.

"I'd rather have rice and beans," Diego said.

"Then you should have bargained for that before you did your little calculations," the man said. "Smoke it or don't, but you need to do a lot of work before morning, and we're not wasting food on a slacker."

The other kids were inhaling the smoke, coughing and weaving a bit, but they were still standing.

"Come on, Diego, I've heard about this. It will give you the strength of ten men."

Diego looked at the cigarette in his hand. "Smoking isn't good for you," he said.

"He's afraid his mamá will find out," Mando said, and Diego felt as if he had been cut with a knife.

Telling himself he was *not* doing it because of what Mando said, Diego leaned into the lantern to light his smoke.

Deborah Ellis

The first breath made his lungs and throat burn, and he wanted to punch the men who had given him this horrible thing. Then he started to feel strangely fine — or was it finely strange? He took another puff, then another.

His hunger became a distant memory, and then it was not even a memory. His body started to burn, but with energy, not pain, and his mind moved fast with glorious thoughts. The notebook in his head flipped its pages. Diego could see they were all full of calculations, and he could understand them all!

"Here you go, boys, into the pit."

Diego's shoes were pulled off, and his pant legs were rolled up as high as they would go. Strong hands helped him climb over the edge of the pit. He laughed at the squishiness of his toes in the mixture of coca leaves and chemicals.

"Don't fall over," someone said, as Diego bumped into a boy who may have been Mando, or it may have been Domingo.

"Let's see how well you dance."

Music came from somewhere — hard-pounding music like the kind Diego would hear from the video game arcades in Cochabamba. The music entered his body and made his feet move up and down, stirring up the leaves and the chemicals, filling his head with smells and sensations.

Time disappeared. One song blended seamlessly into another. Diego's legs kept moving with no effort. He watched his legs being pulled up and down by an invisible puppet master, and he laughed and laughed.

Another cigarette was put to his lips, and a new rush of energy and brilliance zoomed through his body. There was no past and no future. There was only the squish of the coca leaves under his feet.

And then it was morning.

"It's getting light," someone said.

"We're well covered here. And the longer they stomp, the better the stuff. Keep going."

Diego's legs lost their lightness. His head was thick and his whole body ached.

"Give us more smokes?" one of the boys asked.

"You'll be smoking up all the profits. Dance."

Diego kept marching in the pit because to do anything else would have taken too much energy. A cup of water was passed around. He took a drink, then went back to marching.

Finally, they could get out. The bigger men helped them. "We don't want you tripping and spilling this stuff."

Diego joined the other boys on the ground.

"You'll get used to it," Rock said. "They all do."

The men peered into the pit for awhile, discussing something among themselves. Diego leaned against a tree stump and closed his eyes. His stomach was queasy. Nothing felt good.

Something itched on his leg. He put his hand down to scratch it, then let out a scream. Crawling up his leg was the biggest bug he had ever seen. He jumped up and shook his leg, screaming.

The men laughed. Mando was the one who reached out and took the creature off Diego's leg.

"Saved your life again," he said, as they watched the bug crawl away into the underbrush.

"Almost turned you into a girl," Rock taunted.

"I was just surprised," Diego said. "I've never seen one before, not a real one." He was starting to calm down, now that he realized what it was. "It's a rhinoceros beetle. It's harmless. I remember it from science class." He looked in the leaves, found the beetle and picked it up, holding it by the thorax. It was the size of his hand. Its huge black legs and mandibles waved in the air. It really was beautiful.

Rock slapped the beetle out of Diego's hand. It landed on its back, legs going like mad. Rock took aim with his gun, and the loud rat-tat-tat of the machine gun made Diego feel like his body was jumping out of his skin.

"You are the strangest boy in Bolivia," Rock said. "Back to work. We need those leaves fished out. Squeeze all the liquid out of them before you toss them on the pile. Move."

Back into the pit they all went, after washing the dirt from their feet. Instead of marching they bent down, scooped up the mashed coca leaves and tossed them in a pile outside the pit. When all the leaves were out, the men poured more chemicals in, and the boys mixed everything together with their hands and feet. The liquid

Deborah Ellis

stung in a new way, and Diego's back began to hurt from bending over.

Finally, that job was done. Diego and the others were allowed to rest while the men ran a sieve through the liquid, gathering up the gummy resin that had formed in clumps in the pit.

"I hope at least some of you are paying attention," Rock said. "This will be your job tomorrow. We have enough to do without doing your work as well."

The gummy stuff was wrapped in a small piece of foil and placed on a table. The package was the size of a small brick. Diego recognized it. It was the same sort of package the police had found taped under his parents' seat in the minibus.

He helped the men lift some of the stakes holding up the rim of the plastic and watched the chemical soup drain out of the pit and into a nearby stream.

"It's not very much," Rock said, holding up the foil packet. "All those leaves. Are you sure they're stomping it right?"

"It takes two hundred kilos of leaves to produce just one kilo of paste," someone said, "and we need two and a half kilos of paste to make just one kilo of cocaine. That's...kid, how many coca leaves is that?"

"Five hundred kilos," Diego responded, almost without thinking.

"Five hundred kilos of leaves. You think these little city worms you brought us can carry that much through the jungle?"

"They will if we tell them to," Rock said.

"Look at them! Skin and bones! Yell at them all you want, beat them if it makes you happy, but you can't make an ant carry a beetle."

Diego was about to pipe up that ants can carry many times their own weight, but he thought better of it, and kept his mouth shut.

CHAPTER NINE

After they had hiked back to the village, the old woman who ran the tienda had bowls of chupe for the boys, and a place under a tarp where they could sleep protected from the sun. The chupe was good, but the glue boys threw theirs up soon after eating it. Roberto, especially, looked ill, and his hands trembled like leaves in the wind.

"Useless worms you've brought us," one of the men said to Rock, kicking at the glue boys as he walked by with a box of chicha.

The old woman put mugs of coca leaf tea in the glue boys' hands.

"Poor little swallows," she said.

Diego ate his soup, almost too tired to finish

it. He stretched out under the tarp, expecting to fall asleep instantly, but his body wouldn't cooperate. His legs kept twitching, and he had the feeling that he was falling from a long, long way up.

He finally sank into sleep, only to be kicked awake by Rock.

"Time to get up, smart boy. Wake the others. You think we're paying you to sleep?"

At least it's not a buzzer, Diego thought. At least there's no head count.

His whole body ached, including his head, as he got himself moving and woke the others. The glue boys didn't want to get up. Diego did what he could, but in the end it was Rock's kicks that got them to their feet.

They started collecting the coca leaves earlier and got to the pits earlier. Some of the farmers carried sacks of leaves partway down the trail with them, but they were not allowed to go the whole way to the clearing. The boys had to double back to pick up the extra sacks.

Then it was back into the pit. Diego was going to pass on the smoking, because he'd felt so sick when he woke up, but he remembered how much easier it had made the work. He breathed deeply. The smoke brought him back to life, and he started to move.

When the cigarettes came around again, Diego took in as much as his lungs would hold.

"Mamá's boy is growing up," Mando said, and Diego laughed.

He was still buzzing when the sun came up, and he made himself useful straining the clumps of putty out of the chemical solution.

"That's a bit better," Rock said, holding up the slightly larger package of paste. "You may be worth feeding after all."

"Feeding and paying," Diego said.

His sleep that day was even more difficult than the day before. He could not get his brain or his body to rest, so he got up off his mat and went for a walk around the village.

It felt a little funny not to be doing taxi jobs, or rushing to get back to the prison before the doors closed. There was no traffic to dodge, no street gangs to avoid — just green and trees and quiet.

"I can't see this in prison," he said. He'd been too tired and too busy so far to enjoy his freedom.

From now on, he'd pay attention to everything. It would give him something to remember when he was back behind the high stone walls.

He walked around the little village, peeked into the one-room school where a lesson was being taught without books, and chatted with some women who were pounding laundry on the rocks of a stream. He ended up back at the tienda.

"You can't sleep?" the old woman asked him in Spanish. She'd realized that Diego's Aymara vocabulary was limited.

"It's that stuff they give me to smoke."

The old woman nodded. She had a bag of coca leaves in her shop. She pulled one out of the bag.

"This leaf is a gift to my ancestors, the Aymara, and to your ancestors, the Inca, from Pachamama, the mother of our earth. To us it is sacred. It is something we respect and that nurtures us."

She handed the leaf to Diego. He took it gently.

"My parents used to grow coca."

"They have stopped?"

Diego leaned in close to her. "They're in prison," he whispered.

The old woman nodded. "Many of the boys who are brought here to work in the jungle have parents in prison, or not around for some other reason. It's good you know about coca. We have grown and chewed this leaf for centuries. It feeds our bodies, and it is medicine — good for us when we go up into the high mountains where the gringos cannot breathe." She poured hot water from a pot into a mug and added a handful of coca leaves. "You drink this," she said. "It will calm you and help you sleep."

Diego blew on the hot tea to cool it. Mamá made him coca tea in prison when he didn't feel well. Even the scent was familiar and comforting. He took sips while he listened to the old woman talk. She told him tales of the old days, when the world was quieter and people talked directly to the gods.

Maybe it was the tea, maybe it was her voice. Diego fell into a deep sleep and didn't wake up until it was time to rise for work.

Life went on like that for the next few days.

The work was hard and unpleasant, but the drug they were given to smoke made the hours pass quickly. Being busy and tired made it easy to push aside his worries about his family. Things were going well, and he would be back soon, with money.

The best part of each day was being in the village every morning. Mando and the other boys collapsed after eating, but Diego bought an orange soda and sat and talked with the woman who ran the shop, or played football with the little village kids. One day one of the stilt-house families even let him do a few simple chores for them, fetching water and feeding the chickens. It helped him feel normal, and he could go to sleep happy.

"What do you think you're doing, prison boy?" Rock asked, towering over him one morning as he was returning to the space under the tarp after a game of tag with the village kids.

"Going to sleep."

"You're supposed to be sleeping now, not running around the village."

"Just making friends," Diego said.

Rock grabbed his arm. "Giving away our secrets? You're trying to steal our money and our paste, and you're trying to get the locals to help you."

"Let go of me!"

"Or what? Think your new friends will come to your rescue? They've seen dozens of boys like you. They know who their real friends are. Who buys their coca? Who built their school? Our money keeps them quiet."

He let Diego go with a shove. Diego landed in the dirt, almost on top of a sleeping Julio.

"Wake up the other dogs," Rock ordered. "We're heading back to camp."

Diego had to drag the others back from the far, far away place their exhaustion had taken them. Too tired to grumble, they were soon burdened down with sacks of coca, trudging along the jungle trail. The heat and insects formed clouds around them. Little Julio stumbled and had to be pulled up by the others. Rock's mood grew meaner with every step.

By the time they got back to camp, Diego was ready to drop. The glue boys *did* drop, right beside the sacks of coca. Diego sat down on the ground beside them. He realized that their smell no longer bothered him. After a week of sweat and no showers and no clean clothes, he assumed he smelled just as bad.

"Prison boy – clean up this camp."

Diego knew exactly who Rock was talking to. His body felt like lead as he struggled back to his feet.

"Why me? Why do you always ask me? Why don't you get one of the others…" Diego looked around him as he spoke. The three glue boys were sprawled on the ground. Mando was sitting beside Rock, pouring them both a drink of chicha.

Diego stopped complaining. What was the point? He grabbed a trash bag and started picking up the chicha boxes and banana skins the men had scattered around.

The camp consisted of a tent where the men who came and went slept when they had to stay for awhile. Another tent held chemicals and supplies. Folding tables and chairs made up the kitchen and dining area. The little foil bricks of coca paste were stacked neatly on a table in the middle of it all.

Deborah Ellis

Diego swept carefully around the table with a palm leaf. He wondered why the paste, the most valuable thing in the camp, wasn't hidden away. Then he understood. None of the men trusted any of the others. If the coca paste was always in sight, no one would have the opportunity to steal it.

Diego tucked this bit of information away. In prison, the more you knew about the guards, the better off you were. Which guards were mad at each other, which ones were mad at the boss, which ones were homesick, which ones were plain bone mean – all of that knowledge helped the prisoners to know who to avoid and who to flatter.

Diego resolved to keep his eyes open, and he wondered what else he would learn.

Sweat dripped off his forehead, stinging his eyes. He wiped at them with his shirt sleeve, which helped for a moment, but the salt and pressure stung the insect bites on his arm.

His forearm seemed to be swollen. He rolled up his shirt sleeve to get a better look, and let out a cry of horror.

Something was moving inside his arm.

"Get it out! Get it out!" he yelled, not even knowing what it was.

The men looked up from their beer and laughed. Mando jumped to Diego's side, but didn't know how to help.

"Something's in my arm! Get it out!"

"Don't worry, smart boy," Rock laughed. "It will crawl up the inside of your arm, chew up your small brain, then crawl out your eyeballs."

"It won't hurt much!" Paolo laughed.

Diego waved his arm, trying to shake out whatever was living under his skin. The men's laughter grew as he flung himself against the table, sending the foil packets of coca flying around the camp.

Then he knocked against something very big and very solid — something that took hold of his arm with one big, white hand and held it tightly while he made a small, quick cut with a knife. This mountain of a man then took his big hands and squeezed them tight on each side of the writhing lump on Diego's arm. Out of the cut came blood, water and worms, crawling and twisting.

Deborah Ellis

After that, everything went black, as Diego passed out.

He came to a few minutes later, propped up against a table leg while the giant, bald gringo bandaged his arm.

"You were bitten by a sort of a fly," the gringo said in Spanish. His smile was kind, reassuring. The moustache under his nose moved when he talked. "It laid its eggs under your skin, the eggs hatched, and eventually the new flies would have broken through your skin to freedom. But better to have them out now, right?"

Diego nodded. His bandages looked so clean against the filth of his skin. "Thank you."

"Remember, lad, there's nothing in this jungle that you can't eat, or that won't eat you. A jungle is one big feast. Just make sure you're on the eating side of the table!" He pulled Diego to his feet. "Now, pick up those packets. Can't have the profits flung all over the jungle."

Diego scrambled after the packets while the gringo lectured Rock and the others on their stupidity and inefficiency. One of the packets was right by the gringo's feet. Rock strutted, but this man stood, solid and confident. Diego noticed a gun in the holster hanging from his hip.

As quickly as he could, he picked up the packet and added it to the stack on the table, then joined the other boys, sound asleep on the soft, empty coca sacks.

CHAPTER TEN

When Diego opened his eyes, he was staring right at the gringo's thick-soled jungle boots. He was also staring at the butt of a rifle.

"On your feet, lad. Let's go shoot some dinner. What's your name?"

"Diego."

"Well, Diego, call me Smith. These fools have ordered the wrong amount of sulphuric acid, and we won't be able to get any more until tomorrow, so tonight, we feast. How's the arm?"

Diego's arm was better, but Smith didn't seem that interested in an answer. He kept talking.

"When we get back with dinner, we're going to have a little lesson on hygiene in the field. Just because we're in the jungle doesn't mean we're animals, right? Hop to it, lad. One of God's creatures is about to die."

Diego looked around for Mando. He didn't want to go off by himself with this large man with a large gun. But Mando was lighting a cigarette for Rock and not looking up.

Fine, Diego thought.

"I'm coming," he said to Smith.

To his surprise, Diego actually enjoyed himself. They headed off down a trail he didn't know, then they veered off the path. Smith pointed things out to him in a low voice, the way his father had taught him how to spread coca out to dry, or how to plant beans and potatoes.

"I hope you're not ashamed of fainting earlier, or of being afraid," Smith said. "Passing out is just our body's way of giving us a rest, and any man who tells you he's never afraid is a liar. The trick, Diego, is to make fear your friend. Learn to love it. Fear is better than food. Gets your heart pumping, makes you feel alive! I've been afraid for nearly forty years, and I dare you to find anybody who's had a better life."

As they came to an opening in the trees,

Smith put out his arm as a signal to stop. He pointed at the edge of a water-hole. A family of capybaras was taking a drink, their large, round brown bodies bent low over the water. Smith raised his rifle, took one shot, and the jungle seemed to explode. All but one of the capybaras sped off into the bush, and an ocean of birds rose from the trees, squawking. The sound was deafening, but it was exciting, too.

"Hear that, Diego? Can't find a noise that pretty in Manhattan. Come on!"

The dead capybara was on the far shore of the little pond. Smith handed Diego the rifle. "Shoot anything that comes near me," he said, as he waded into the water. Diego raised the rifle like he had seen Smith do. It was heavier than he had imagined it would be. It made him feel bigger. He watched Smith heave the giant rodent over his shoulder and wade back.

"Feels like a hundred pounder," Smith said. "I've seen them twice this size. Lead the way back to camp, Diego. Let's see how good a tracker you are. See if you can find signs of where we've been."

Diego turned around. At first the jungle

looked like a big green mess, a chaos with no pattern. Then he spotted part of a footprint in the mud, and some broken branches. Bit by bit, and with Smith's occasional help, Diego led them back to the trail.

At camp, Smith shouted out orders for firewood, for a spit to be built, and a pit dug for the carcass outside camp. "While you're at it, dig some latrines. What distinguishes men from beasts? Toilets."

Diego and the other boys worked hard, but so did the men, who looked a lot less happy about it.

"Go wash," Smith ordered. "I'm not feasting with a bunch of stinkers. Your smell will ruin the taste of the food." He made the men fetch water and clean clothes from among their own belongings so that the boys could wash theirs. Bars of soap appeared. "No excuse for being dirty," Smith said. "You can take a bath with half a cup of water if you have to." He kept up a steady stream of advice and orders while he skinned, gutted and butchered the capybara. The smell of roasting meat soon filled the camp.

The sun went down, and everyone feasted.

Boxes of chicha were passed around, and the capybara meat was tender and good.

"This reminds me of Cambodia," Smith said. "Jungle just as thick, but even more deadly because it was crawling with Commies as well as snakes. Nothing like a feast in the jungle, enemies all around, death at every snapping twig. It's like partying during the plague, the last meal before execution, that last cigarette before a battle. Is anything again ever so sweet?"

Smith lapsed into silence, but only for a moment. "I envy you boys, just now discovering all the things I've grown used to. That freshness, that sense of wonder! Turning your backs on soft city living! I want you boys to get excited, to grab onto life with both hands!"

Smith slapped Julio on the back in a good-natured way, but Julio almost fell over, even though he was sitting down. Smith didn't notice. He kept on talking.

"Even this is fancier than I'm used to. Try making heroin in the rainforests of Laos! Try escaping from a drug lord's private jail in Afghanistan! Oh, the things I've done to keep my countrymen stoned and stupid. Even given up my name. Do you know the story of Rumpel-stiltskin?" Smith kept talking without giving anyone a chance to reply. "Ugly little dwarf, spun straw into gold. Well, that's what I'm doing here. Weeds into gold, lads. Weeds into gold."

"Coca is not a weed," Diego spoke, his mouth acting before his brain, again. "Coca is a gift to the Inca and the Aymara from Pachamama, from Mother Earth, to keep us well and strong."

"Ah, local myths and legends. I respect that. Now here's one for you. Comes straight from the mouth of our Lord. A man had three sons, gave them each a gift. The oldest son tripled the value of that gift, the middle son doubled it, and the youngest son buried his in the ground. Your people have had the gift of coca for thousands of years, and what have you done with it? Chewed it and made tea. First the Spaniards fed it to you so that you could work without complaint or pay in the silver mines of Potosí, and now we gringos have turned it into an empire, the Empire of Cocaine. Weeds into an empire. Straw into gold. No wonder we run the world."

Smith kept talking, switching from cocaine to running guns in Nicaragua, to killing people in places Diego had never heard of. Diego left the fire and lay down out of Smith's eyesight. Mando joined him.

They lay quietly for a moment, listening to Smith drone on and on, like the woman in prison who always talked to herself.

"He's loco," Diego whispered.

"Sure, loco, but also rich," said Mando.

Diego turned his back to his friend and tried to sleep. He wanted to dream about kind people, so that he wouldn't forget that they still existed.

He awoke during the night to a strange sensation around his ankles — kind of a tickling and kind of a nibbling. He put his hand down to scratch, then sat up with a start.

Bats were crawling around him, on feet that were not really feet. They joined other bats, feeding on the legs of the boys.

Diego sprang to his feet and waved them away. Bat wings filled the air. Diego went from boy to boy, wiping away trickles of blood and covering their bare legs with any bits of cloth he could find.

"Vampire bats," a soft voice said. Smith was

wide awake, sitting alone in the dark, watching the boys sleep, watching the bats feast. "Just like Dracula."

Diego lay back down, close to his friend. Mando was whimpering in his sleep. Diego put his arm around him, to protect them both from the monsters of the night.

CHAPTER ELEVEN

"What happens to that?" Diego asked the next morning, nodding at the stack of foil packets on the table.

"None of your business," snarled Rock.

"Don't be like that," Smith said. "Diego is a smart kid. Maybe he wants to learn the business."

"Maybe," Diego said.

"Good answer. Don't give a lot away. These packets get taken to a laboratory outside Bolivia, where the paste is further refined and turned into that white powder that my countrymen are so eager to shove up their noses. And all along the way, people get rich."

"That's why I'm here," Diego said.

"Drugs are the way to do it," Smith said. "Drugs buy guns, guns buy people, and when you buy people, you can buy power."

"Power for what?" Diego asked.

"For whatever you want. Isn't there something you would like?"

"He'd like to get his mommy and daddy out of prison," Rock said in a mocking voice, but that was exactly what Diego did want.

"With enough power, you can buy your own prison," Smith said. "Wouldn't you like to lock away your enemies? With enough power, you can even buy a president."

"A president of Bolivia?" Diego had a vague image of a man in a suit. What would he do with a president?

"Not Bolivia. The campesinos are too organized here. Every time they don't like something, they protest and shut the country down. No, you'd want to buy a president of a country where people are too poor and too scared to know what's going on, or too rich and busy watching television to care."

Smith looked at his watch. "Supplies should

be coming in soon." He took two of the men and went down a trail.

There was cold rice and leftover meat for breakfast. Diego scooped some food onto a palm leaf and joined the other boys. They were staring at something on the ground. Diego looked, too.

A parade of ants was going by. Each one carried a leaf five times its size. Julio put a rock in their path. The ants were confused for a moment, then continued on their way.

The boys watched the ants for awhile before they turned back to their food. Smith had ordered the men to be sure the boys got enough to eat, and to let them drink whenever they were thirsty.

"We've got gringo legs," Roberto said, "and hands." The chemicals were bleaching the natural brown color out of their skin, leaving a washed-out white. White and red, actually, because of the blisters and sores that stood out against their pale, wrinkled skin.

"You're spending a lot of time with Rock," Diego said quietly to Mando. "What are you doing?"

"He's got it all," Mando said. "Money, power. He takes orders only from Smith, and one day he'll be even richer than the gringo. He's a good guy. You should give him a chance."

"These are not nice people," Diego said. "Rock is like a bully in the prison, and Smith is like a prison guard."

"They're businessmen, tycoon, just like you and me."

"We are *not* like them!"

"Well, maybe we should be!" Mando replied. "Who would you rather be like — these guys?" He jerked his head at the glue boys, who moved from smoke to sleep. "Like our parents, stuck in a cage? Or like Smith and Rock? They have money. If we stick with them, we'll have money, too."

"I haven't seen any money yet," Diego said. "You said we were going to get rich on this job. Well, the job is half over. I'd like to know just how rich I'm going to be."

The other boys were listening. They wanted to know about the money, too.

"They'll pay us when they're ready," Mando said, but he didn't sound so sure.

148   *Deborah Ellis*

"Go ask them when that will be. Rock is such a good guy. Go ask him."

"All right. I will." Mando got to his feet. Diego went with him.

Rock was sitting at the table with the other men, drinking chicha.

"Excuse me, Rock," Mando said, keeping his voice casual. "My friends and I were wondering about our pay."

"What about it?"

Mando didn't seem to know what to say next.

"Well," Diego said, "we want to know how much we'll get, and when we'll get it, and when we're going back to Cochabamba."

Rock lit a cigarette. "You want to know how much you're getting. You don't ask about how much you owe us."

Diego was stunned. "We don't owe you anything!"

"Ten days of food and shelter, transportation from Cochabamba, and all that coca paste you've smoked. Somebody has to pay for that."

Diego looked around for the other boys. He wanted them to join him. He wanted to feel backed up, even if they didn't say anything. But they stayed where they were. Even Mando had taken a step back.

"How much are we getting?" Diego asked again.

"We'll have to figure that out, won't we? How much do you think you are worth?"

The other men joined in. "Prison trash asking about their wages? How much did you sign on for, boy?"

At that moment, Diego realized his grave mistake. As a taxi, he *never* took a job before settling on what it would pay, and what exactly he would have to do. He'd leapt into this job blindly, without even thinking to ask.

"We were promised good wages," he said. "We would like those wages now, whatever is coming to us up to this point. You can pay us the rest when the job is done."

"You're after my money, aren't you, smart boy, just like I said you would be." Rock stepped forward and pointed his gun at Diego's head. Diego saw Smith and the other men come back into the clearing, loaded down with containers of chemicals.

"I don't want *your* money," Diego stressed,

Deborah Ellis

keeping his voice calm. "I just want *my* money, what I've earned, what we've all earned."

"And what do you think you'll spend it on, out here in the jungle?" the men laughed.

"We'd just like to have it, you know, because we're boys, and we'd like to pretend we're rich." I am not a threat to you, Diego told them in his mind, but neither am I going to back down.

"You'd like to pretend you're rich." Again, the idiotic laughter.

Diego smiled and looked back at the other boys, to get them to smile as well. "You know, like we'll all buy bicycles and fancy clothes and ride around Cochabamba looking like big shots. We want to impress the girls."

The men laughed again. Some made obscene gestures. Diego pretended not to notice.

He spoke over their laughter, as friendly and as respectful as he could be. "So, if it's all the same to you, we'd like our money now."

The firmness in Diego's face and voice stopped their laughter.

"We don't have your money now," Smith said. "First we sell the coca paste. Then we pay you."

Diego saw all kinds of problems with that. Would the boys have to hang around the jungle until the paste was sold? How long would that be? Would they have to keep paying for their food and shelter while they waited? If they went back to Cochabamba without being paid, would the men come to the prison to pay them?

No, it was no good. He was a businessman. He'd lost his mind for awhile, but he had it back now, and he wasn't about to be lied to.

"He has money," Diego said, nodding at Rock. The barrel of the gun came closer. "He paid the farmers, and he can pay us. You can pay him back when you sell the paste."

"The cocaleros are organized," Rock said. "They have a union. We have to pay them. You have nothing. You are nothing. We could shoot you, dump you in the jungle, and by dawn your bones would be stripped clean. Nobody knows where you are, and no one will care if you disappear."

"And you would lose a good worker," Diego said. He was way beyond being scared. Rock could easily carry out his threat, and that would be that. Diego could meet that fate a lot more easily than he could go back to his mother empty-handed. "It would not be good business. Good business is when everybody wins."

"Put the gun down," Smith said to Rock. "We are not generally in the business of shooting boys. We are in the business of making cocaine. You'll have your money when the work is done and we decide to pay you." He turned away, barking orders about where the chemicals should be stored.

Diego went back to the other boys. He was still alive, but there was no money bulging in his pockets. The others started sweeping the old coca leaves into the jungle. They didn't look at him. Not even Mando would look at him.

Diego didn't have any money, but he did have answers. They just weren't the answers he wanted.

And the worst part was that it was his own fault.

It was time to stop being so stupid, and time to start being a taxi again, watching for dangers, watching for opportunities, and watching for his chance to come out ahead.

CHAPTER TWELVE

The more attention Diego paid, the more he noticed. It helped that Smith had them stomping coca during the day, too, with just a couple of hours of rest between refilling the pits. It meant that Diego was awake during the day to see things.

He noticed that men came and went on different trails from the one he and the other boys took from the village. Some men were less tired and sweaty when they arrived, and their clothes were cleaner. That meant their trail must be shorter.

All roads led somewhere. All trails would lead somewhere, too. That was the point of having a trail, to get from one place to another.

He paid attention to the stream, which brought

water to the camp and took away the chemical sludge from the paste-making. A stream, like a trail, went from one place to another. It was another way out.

He noticed the packages of coca paste, tightly wrapped in foil, stacked neatly on a table. The pile grew every day.

A wild, crazy idea began to take hold in his head. The more he tried to shake it loose, the more firmly it held on.

"They're not going to pay us," he whispered to Mando when they were both off in the bush gathering firewood. It was hard to have a conversation that wasn't noticed or overheard.

"They will," Mando said, but not very firmly.

"Who will we complain to if they don't? Nobody. So it's on us. We can't go back to Cochabamba empty-handed."

"I'm not going back at all," Mando said.

That surprised Diego. "You have to go back. Your father will worry."

"My father is in prison! I don't want to go back to living in a cell. I'm going to stay with Rock, help them carry the coca paste out of the country to the lab."

"Have they asked you to do that?"

"No, but they will." Again, his voice was not very sure.

"We've always stuck together," Diego said.

"Do you have a better suggestion, tycoon?"

"We steal the paste," Diego said.

Mando dropped the wood he was carrying. He almost shouted, but stopped himself in time.

"Do you want to be shot?"

"We can do it if we're smart. We won't take all of it, just a pack or two. If they can sell it, so can we."

"I ought to turn you in. I ought to tell them your plan."

"I'm not going back to the prison without money."

"And I'm not going back to the prison at all."

"What are you ladies doing in the bush?" Rock shouted from the camp. "Did you find a romantic little spot?"

"We're getting wood," Diego shouted back. To Mando, he whispered, "We don't know how much longer we'll be here. Once all the coca is stomped, the men could take off and we'll never see them again, or our money. Just think about it."

156   *Deborah Ellis*

"Keep away from me," Mando said. "And keep away from that paste. I've found a place for myself. I have a future with these guys. Don't ruin it for me."

They went back to the camp and endured dumb jokes from the men. Diego found himself missing school. At least the idiots there had someone to shut them up occasionally.

Days went by. The stomping became harder as their feet became covered with sores from the chemicals. Even Diego cried out when the chemicals first hit his blisters at the beginning of a work session, before the drugged cigarettes dulled the pain.

Smith came and went from the camp. He berated Rock and the others for their lack of progress.

"My other pits are producing twice the paste you are! If you want to keep your jobs, you'll step it up." Rock's idea of stepping it up was to yell louder at the boys.

Diego continued to make himself useful. The glue boys didn't have it in them to do anything but smoke, stomp and sleep. Some of the men took to taunting them at night, holding the paste cigarettes just out of their reach so they'd beg for them. Diego spoke up for them one night, so the men made him stomp the coca leaves without any of the drug. That night was long and hard. He couldn't take his mind off the pain in his feet.

Still, the next day, he forced himself to do extra chores again. He'd seen men and women in the prisons who gave up, who stopped washing or working or doing anything to make their lives better. A deadness took over their eyes and eventually their faces and whole bodies.

So Diego did chores for the men he'd come to hate. He pounded their laundry upstream from where the chemicals were dumped, and spread their clothes in the sun to dry. He kept the kettle full of water, and kept the yard swept.

"You'll make somebody a good wife," the men joked. Diego let the laughter bounce off him, and took note that the man Smith put in charge of guarding the packages of coca paste had trouble staying awake in the heat of the day.

Everything he did helped him learn a little more, and everything he learned helped him feel a little stronger.

Bit by bit, the stack of sacks full of coca leaves

was getting smaller. The work was getting harder, though. The coca paste cigarettes didn't have the power they first had to make everything bad disappear. Diego tried to push away thoughts of his parents worrying about him, but as the days went by, that was getting harder, too. By now his mother would have learned that he wasn't staying with his father. She would be imagining all sorts of terrible things.

Smith put an end to the music, saying it gave him a headache. For awhile he entertained them with stories of jungle warfare, tales of bloodshed and violence that he told with relish, as though he were describing a great meal or a vacation.

"You can stay alive easily in a jungle," he said. "Lots of things to kill, lots of things to eat. You boys are so lucky, getting to live rough like this while you are still young, not having to put up with school clubs and orthodontists and parents who worry if you don't eat your vegetables! You're being treated like men out here, not babies!"

Diego didn't understand half of what Smith was saying. He was glad when the man finally shut up about knifing people and setting booby traps with sharpened bamboo, but there was nothing to relieve the tedium of the work. The closer they came to the end, the edgier the men all seemed to be. There were fewer dumb jokes and more stupid arguments.

"Everybody shut up!" Smith bellowed one night, three and a half weeks into the job. "Listen!"

The rhythmic thump-thump-thump of a helicopter was coming closer and closer.

"Douse those lights!"

Lamps were put out, and water was splashed onto the cookfire. The boys bumped against each other in the sudden darkness. Diego felt somebody slip and fall.

The helicopter noise got louder. The trees above had broad, thick branches, but Diego could still see the spotlight, searching for people doing just what they were doing.

When the helicopter had passed, Diego heard somebody spit in disgust. It was Rock.

"Trying to keep decent people from earning a living," he said.

"That's just what you're doing by not paying us," Diego said.

"I'll pay you with bullets," Rock snarled.

"Okay, okay, let's get the lamps on and get back to work," Smith said. "Cocaine used to be legal. They put it in Coca-Cola! The Pope put it in his wine. And now we have to hide in the jungle like animals. Get those lamps lit!"

Diego heard the men stumble around, finding matches, and bit by bit, the small clearing had light again.

The sight that greeted them was not good.

Mando had slipped, crushing the plastic wall of the pit. Gallons of the solution were spilling out.

"On your feet!" Rock roared, rushing over and kicking Mando.

"My ankle..." Diego heard his friend say. He helped Mando untangle himself from the plastic and took him away from the pit. Rock followed, yelling and hitting them with the butt of his machine gun. Not even Smith stopped him.

"Get this cleaned up," Smith ordered, when Rock had tired of hitting. "You're in charge of these kids, Rock. Any losses are coming out of your share."

The pit was repaired, the dirt was washed off

the boys' feet, and back they went into the chemicals and leaves. Mando had hurt his ankle, and he leaned against Diego while they stomped.

There were no more friendly conversations between Rock and Mando, no more drinking chicha together, no more lessons on how to clean the machine gun. Rock ignored him altogether.

Given who and what Rock was, Diego felt that Mando had got off lucky.

CHAPTER THIRTEEN

"We need more firewood," Rock declared two days later. "Smart boy, go get some."

"I'll go with you," Mando offered. "Two can carry twice as much as one."

Rock waved them into the bush. It was a quiet day at the camp. Smith had gone to check on one of his other coca pits. Some of the men had gone for supplies. Most of the others were asleep in the tent. The glue boys were crashed out on the ground, sleeping in the dirt.

"All right, I'm with you," Mando whispered, as they picked their way carefully through the underbrush. His ankle was sore, but better. "Do you have a plan?"

"It would be better for us if they didn't know

they'd been robbed." Diego told him what he'd been thinking. They could wrap some dirt up in foil, making a fake package of coca paste, and somehow put the fake one on the pile and sneak the real one away.

"What about the other boys? We have to include them."

Diego wasn't so sure. "The more people in on a secret, the more chance it will get out. Plus, they don't seem able to carry out a plan." He picked up a piece of dead wood to add to his bundle. Staring up at him was a spider, as hairy as a dog and as big as a dinner plate. It waved its front arms at Diego as if to say, "Put that wood back!"

Mando laughed and picked the creature up. Its legs hung over the edges of his open palm.

"It's a tarantula," he said. "It won't hurt you. Well, it might hurt you, but it won't kill you. I saw a guy in Cochabamba showing these off in the street. He had a little spider circus, made them ride in swings, go down a little slide. He told me all about them." Mando held it out toward Diego. "Touch it."

Slowly, Diego moved his fingers forward until they stroked the hair on the spider's back

Deborah Ellis

"I think I'd rather have a dog," he said.

"The man told me it's the little spiders you have to watch out for," Mando said. "They're the ones that can kill you." He lowered the tarantula to the ground to let it go. But Diego had an idea.

"Let's keep him. He may come in handy." He took his handkerchief out of his pocket and opened it. "Put him in here."

Mando handed him the spider, and Diego tied the corners of the cloth together so it couldn't get out.

"We'll hide it at the edge of the camp until we need it."

Diego believed what his friend had told him about the huge spider not being poisonous, but he didn't like the thought of it crawling on him, and he wouldn't like to be surprised by it. He imagined the men in the camp would feel the same.

At the edge of the camp, they stopped.

"Let's leave our friend here," Diego said. He put down the firewood to free his arms and used a stick to brush away some leaves. "We'll hide it here. I'll put a marker over it so we'll know how to find it."

Mando, his arms aching, headed into the camp to put the wood he had collected on the woodpile. Diego made a circle in the leaves, put the tied handkerchief in the middle and piled leaves on top. Then he arranged some sticks in a pyramid on top of it all. He hoped the spider would be all right in there.

He picked up his firewood again, straightened up, and looked right into the barrel of Rock's machine gun.

"Hiding something, smart boy?"

"What would we have to hide?" Diego asked. He shifted the firewood in his arms, hoping to cover up the sound of his heart thumping in his chest.

Rock knocked the wood out of Diego's arms.

"I'm on to you, smart boy. Always watching, always doing your little jobs, making everyone think you're so useful. Well, I've got you now." He kicked over Diego's pyramid. Keeping the gun pointed at Diego, Rock knelt down, brushed away the leaves, and found the hand-kerchief.

"Not hiding anything, eh? What do you call this?"

"It's just personal stuff," Diego said, his voice casual.

"I think you've been stealing from us, and now I have the proof. I hope you like the jungle, smart boy, because your bones will be spending eternity here." Rock picked up the handkerchief and nodded for Diego to go ahead of him into the camp.

As they came into the clearing, Diego could see Mando out of the corner of his eye. Mando grasped the situation instantly, and moved casually over to the folding table, to the stack of coca-paste packages.

"What's this?" one of the men asked, frowning.

"I caught him stealing. He was hiding this in the underbrush. He's probably got stashes all over this camp."

The other men in the clearing gathered around Rock. They looked down at Diego.

"Are you stealing from us, boy?"

"Do we kill him now or wait until Smith gets back?"

Diego saw Mando slip one of the packets off the table. He held it down by his side a moment, then dropped it down his shirt.

At the same moment, Rock untied the hand-kerchief. The tarantula, angry at being trapped and bounced around, leapt out and onto Rock's face.

Rock screeched. Diego started to run but was grabbed by one of the other men. Mando lobbed firewood and coca packets at the men's heads and took off as soon as they let go of Diego to defend themselves.

"Run!" Mando yelled, zooming off down a trail. Diego plunged into the bush after him, moving his legs as fast as they would go.

"I'm right behind you," he yelled. "Keep going!"

Suddenly, the jungle stopped. The ground dropped away into a canyon. All that stood between them and the river far, far below was a bridge made of rope and a narrow strip of planks tied together. Some of the planks were missing.

"Saved your life again, tycoon," Mando called back, jumping onto the bridge. It swung wildly with every step he took.

"Be careful!" Diego hollered.

Mando turned around and let go of the guide

rope – maybe to show off, maybe to wave. Diego never knew.

For a long, terrible moment, Diego watched his friend waver, almost hover in the air, as if he was waiting for the Angel Gabriel to swoop down from heaven and carry him away.

But the Angel was sleeping, again, and Diego's friend tumbled over the rope railing, and fell down, down and away.

"Mando!" Diego screamed, darting out to the edge of the ridge, his feet slipping and fumbling in the soft earth and loose stones. He saw his friend's body smashed on the river boulders deep in the canyon. It seemed to Diego that he could easily join Mando there, and he didn't care.

Then he felt the strong, wide hands of Smith gripping his shoulders, pulling him back from death, and along the trail to the camp.

CHAPTER FOURTEEN

Crying and shaking, images of Mando's father waiting by the prison door, of Mando saving Diego's life and Diego not being able to return the gift. Someone put a blanket around Diego's shoulders and he dropped to the dirt, curling up around his pain and wanting the dirt to cover him up in darkness.

"There's a packet missing."

"Of course there is," Smith said. "Why else would they be running?"

Diego was lifted to his feet. Rock raised an arm to slap him, but Diego was faster. He rammed himself head first into Rock's belly and, with a whoosh of air from his lungs, Rock was on the ground.

Deborah Ellis

"This was supposed to be a job, just a stupid job!"

Rock sprang back to his feet and came at Diego with full force, his face grotesque with rage, but Smith stepped between them.

"We already have one dead boy," Smith said. "Corpses interfere with business. Start breaking camp."

"He stole from us!"

"Don't you worry about him." Diego felt Smith's fingers digging into his shoulder. "He's ours now. He'll make good. Pack up."

Rock snorted, but he couldn't disobey Smith. Smith bent down and looked at Diego, eyeball to eyeball.

"You took something of mine."

Diego didn't blink. He owed this man nothing.

"Is it still in the camp? Or is it floating down the river with your friend's body?"

Diego's eyes teared up again.

"That's just as I thought." Smith ruffled Diego's hair, then took hold of his arm and didn't let go as he moved around the camp giving orders. The tents were taken down, the packages of coca paste were packed into a suitcase, and anything of value was piled up at the entrance to one of the trails.

All through this activity, Julio, Domingo and Roberto sat cowering on the edge of the clearing.

It didn't take the men long to get their things together. The clearing was a mess of garbage, torn tarp, plastic jugs and buckets. It was a garbage dump, not a rain forest. It looked like a handful of jungle had been stomped on.

"You'll take care of them?" Smith asked Rock, nodding at the glue boys.

"As usual."

"You're not going to kill them!" Diego twisted in vain to get away from Smith's grip. "Run!" he yelled to the other boys, but the boys just sat, too frightened and confused to move.

"Calm down, Diego. He's not going to kill them. You have my word." Smith's word didn't mean anything to Diego, and that mistrust must have shown in his face. Smith bent down again to talk to him. "As I've already said, we're not in the business of killing boys. They'll be driven back to Cochabamba, given enough money for a few pots of glue, and will soon be back to sleeping on their garbage dump. They probably won't even remember this, and if they do, nobody will believe them. We don't need to kill them."

"Let me go back, too," Diego pleaded. "I want to go back to Cochabamba with them. I promise not to remember a thing! No one will find out about you." He kept squirming, even though he knew it was no use.

"Cochabamba is such a dreary city," Smith said. "We've got something much better in mind for you. Where's your adventurous spirit?"

Diego opened his mouth and started to scream, because there was nothing left he could do.

Smith's hand moved from his arm to his mouth.

"You'll scare the wildlife. A lot of endangered species here," he said calmly. "And you'll give me a headache. So stop that noise or I'll rip out your tonsils."

Diego stopped. There was no point to it anyway. He watched in utter misery as Rock and Paolo ordered the glue boys onto the trail. Julio was the only one able to turn back and wave at

Diego before Rock's rough shove made him disappear into the thick of the trees.

Only two of the men remained behind with Diego and Smith. One of them picked up the suitcase, but Smith, still clutching Diego with one hand, took it from him.

"Let's go," he said. He led the way, dragging Diego. The men followed with the last of their property.

Twenty minutes down another trail, the forest opened up to a long strip of cleared land. Trees had been chopped down, and the afternoon sun shone on a smooth length of grass. Smith put the suitcase full of coca paste on the ground between his feet and lit a cigarette. The air buzzed with cicadas. Diego felt very, very tired.

"Where am I going?" he asked, not really expecting an answer.

"Where would you like to go?" Smith replied in an almost jovial voice. "New York City? San Francisco?"

Diego remembered the posters of the long bridge and the crowded city.

"Cochabamba," he said.

Smith laughed. "I'm glad you'll be with us for

awhile longer," he said. "I've really come to like you. Most stomping boys are too stupid or too drugged out to talk back. And here's an important lesson for you. Make the drugs, sell the drugs, become rich from the drugs, but don't use the drugs. Let others destroy their brain cells."

"That's good advice, boss," one of the men said.

"I should go on the lecture circuit," Smith said. "Just like Kissinger, right, Diego? Just like Dr. Phil."

"If you like me, you should let me go home."

"Can't do it, son," Smith said. "Can't bear to think of you living in that prison again and missing this opportunity to see the world. Besides, you have to pay back what you stole. We're going to strap cocaine to that tiny chest of yours and send you up to feed all the hungry noses in America."

In the distance, Diego heard the thump-thump of a helicopter propeller.

Soldiers! They were his best chance now. He kept talking, trying to distract Smith from the sound. If they came close enough, maybe he could run out in the field and signal to them.

"I don't have a passport," he said. He knew a

bit about traveling. "And the plane ride will be expensive. I don't think you would make much money by sending me north. But I do a good business in Cochabamba. I work as a taxi, and I have a homework service. I could pay you back that way."

The helicopter was getting closer.

"I told you this was a bright boy," Smith said to his men. "You'll have to watch your backs. He'll be after your jobs!"

Then Diego saw the helicopter appear over the tree tops. In a burst of energy, he yanked himself away from Smith and ran out into the clearing, waving his arms.

"I'm here! I'm here! Help me!" he yelled. He didn't look back, sure Smith and the others were close behind, or were raising their guns to shoot him. He kept running and waving.

A massive wind swirled up dust and debris around him as the helicopter landed. He reached it just as the door was opening.

"Help me!" he screamed above the noise of the engine. "They're drug makers! They're taking me away!"

"That's right, Diego," said Smith, right

behind him again, speaking directly into his ear. "We're taking you away."

Diego saw then that the pilot was not in a uniform. Smith's men opened the back of the helicopter and loaded in the things from the camp. They got in, too. Then Smith pulled Diego up beside him. They sat by the open door, legs dangling out. Diego held onto whatever he could find, but was horrified to feel the helicopter lurch and see the ground drop away.

"Isn't this better than living in the prison?" Smith asked. "Stick with me, kid, and I'll show you the world. Money, power, you can have it all. I like your spirit."

In spite of his fear, Diego was captivated by the sight below. So much green! Endless forest, thick and dark, so unlike Cochabamba's red earth mountains. This was Bolivia, his country, the land of his ancestors. It had been given to them by Pachamama, the same way coca had been given to them, to be cared for and respected. It did not belong to this gringo, who wanted only to drain it of all that was good.

Smith's big hand grabbed hold of the back of Diego's neck.

"It's a big jungle," he said. "Can swallow a man whole."

Smith tightened his fingers into Diego's flesh. Diego shut his eyes and prepared to die, then opened them again. If he was going to die, he wanted to see it coming.

"I am God," Smith said. "Serve me well, and I will bless you. Curse me, and you will find yourself in hell."

He kept his hand on Diego's neck, but he did not push him out. They soared over the tall trees and river valleys, into a green that did not end. It was magnificent, and terrible, and Diego was so exhausted and scared that he no longer distinguished between the two.

After a time, the ground began to get closer, and Diego saw they were aiming for a small clearing with several buildings. Soon the helicopter was on the ground, and Smith and Diego were on their feet.

"Did you like that?" Smith asked, as the propellers slowed to silence. "One day you, too, could have your own helicopter. Or maybe you'd like a plane instead."

Men came out of the buildings to greet them.

Deborah Ellis

"I've brought us a first-class courier," Smith said. "Treat him well." He handed Diego over to one of the new men, then turned to get the suitcase of coca paste out of the helicopter.

For that one moment, no one clutched him, and Diego took full advantage, plunging headlong into the jungle.

CHAPTER FIFTEEN

✳

A spray of machine-gun fire followed Diego into the bush. Birds rose up from the trees, and their shrieking propelled him forward. He scrambled over fallen logs, smacked into trees, tore through barbed vines, and tripped over things he couldn't see.

When he finally stopped running, he tried to calm his panting so that he could hear if he was still being followed. The birds and monkeys were settling down. He didn't hear any footsteps, but he didn't know if he would. Would they be able to sneak up on him? Would the jungle hide the sounds he made? Diego didn't wait around to find out. He started moving again.

On and on he went, not knowing if he was

Deborah Ellis

going in a straight line, if he was going away from trouble or into more.

He kept moving until his legs simply wouldn't move any farther. He tried to climb over a large log, but found he didn't have the strength. He sank down to the floor of the forest.

He was so thirsty! The air in the forest seemed to be sucking all the moisture out of him. All the water in his body was on the outside of him, not inside, where it belonged. He leaned his head back to rest it against the log.

In the next instant, he was on his feet again, shrieking in pain. He forced himself into silence, but something was sticking little knives in him all over his body.

Tiny creatures were crawling on him. Diego did a crazy dance, hopping around and slapping himself, trying to brush the fire ants from his skin without getting more bites. He jumped and spun and bumped blindly into a tree. He looked up to grab a vine to steady himself, then snatched his arm back again – he was about to grab onto the swinging end of a very large snake.

Finally, the bugs were off him, and there was nothing left to do but cry. He couldn't pretend any more that he was brave. He was tired of being strong and looking after business. He wanted his mother to be there, to take care of things, and to bring Mando back.

"Diego."

The sob stifled itself in Diego's throat. He looked up, but all he could see was jungle.

"Diego. Don't cry, son. Everything will be fine."

It was Smith.

Diego sprang to his feet and spun around, looking in every direction. No Smith. But he was there.

"You remind me of myself when I was young," Smith said. "Tough. Of course, there were no jungles in Wisconsin, where I grew up. There used to be a forest. I hunted there with my father and grandfather. Now it's a shopping mall."

Diego couldn't make any sense of what Smith was saying. He took off again, running away from where he thought Smith's voice was coming from.

He ran and ran, until his chest ached and his legs burned with pain, pushing himself to the

Deborah Ellis

point of exhaustion, stopping when he could go no farther.

"Diego."

He heard Smith's voice again.

"Where do you think you're going to run? I've been hunting people in one jungle or another since I was eighteen. There are a lot of things in a jungle that can kill you. You really have to watch your step."

A single rifle shot sounded. Diego jumped and started running again.

"I'm getting too old for this," Smith called out. "I should just leave you out here to die, but I don't like loose ends. Loose ends are not professional." He shot again, but Diego was already out of the range of his rifle.

Diego didn't know how he kept moving. With every step, he expected to die, killed by a bullet or a snake or a creature he didn't even know about.

Smith kept talking to him as they moved through the bush.

"You could have had a great future with us," Smith called out. "We were going to make you into a courier, running drugs across the border,

I Am a Taxi   183

maybe even all the way into Canada. Wouldn't you like to see Toronto? Go to a hockey game?"

Diego kept moving. If he gave up, no one would ever know what had happened to him. Even if he went back to the prison with empty hands, at least his family wouldn't be left with a big question mark in their lives.

A series of small logs had fallen over a pond, giving Diego a bridge to scamper over. He hopped from one mossy, slippery log to another. Most were big and solid. One was skinny and unstable. It bobbed and shook under his weight, but he got off it quickly and made it to the other side.

Smith's voice was getting closer and closer. Diego dashed up a small ridge overlooking the pond.

And couldn't go any farther.

His foot was stuck.

He had stepped into a hole, or a tangle of roots. He pulled and yanked, tears of panic soaking his face as Smith appeared on the other side of the pond.

"I guess my eyesight's not what it used to be," Smith said, his voice calm, as if he were buying onions in the market. "All those years as a sniper. I could put a bullet between the eyes of one of Ho Chi Minh's comrades from a quarter of a mile away. Old age — it's not for sissies!" Smith laughed. He began to cross the log bridge.

"These days, of course, I usually get others to do my killing. Remember what I told you about power? But I'm a better shot than the others. I'll be able to kill you without wounding you. I've developed a fondness for you, Diego, and I don't want you to suffer. A clean kill is a gift to an enemy you respect."

Smith was halfway across the pond, moving slowly. Diego was trapped. There was no need to hurry.

"Why kill me at all?" Diego asked. "I'll probably die out here anyway."

"Yes, but a slow, painful death. I'm not a monster, Diego. I like to think of myself as a father figure to all you throwaway boys who make your way to my cocaine pits."

Smith raised his rifle. Diego bent this way and that, moving as much as he could so Smith couldn't get a fix on him in his rifle-sight. Then

Diego picked up whatever he could get his hands on — sticks, rocks, dirt — and threw them down on the big American.

"Hold still! You want me to wound you?" Smith recoiled from a stone that hit him on his bald head, drawing blood. He moved closer to get a better shot.

He stepped onto the skinny, wobbly log. His balance failed him. He tried to retrieve it, but the log rolled underneath him, and his feet did a brief, crazy dance to try to stay on top of it.

It was no good. He went into the water. His rifle landed on a patch of sand not far away, on the edge of the pond.

The water was not very deep. Smith's head surfaced as he regained his footing.

"Nothing like a dunking on a hot day," he laughed, as he waded through the water toward his gun.

Diego wiggled his foot and pulled. It was coming loose.

Smith was almost within reach of his rifle. This close to Diego, he wouldn't miss. There wasn't much time.

Diego kept pulling on his foot.

Smith reached the sand bank. Two more steps, and he would have his gun. And then...

"Diego!"

Diego looked up. Smith's legs had sunk into the wet sand past his knees. The rifle was just beyond his reach.

"Toss me a branch or a vine," Smith ordered. "You help me, I'll help you. That's good business."

Diego didn't waste time answering. One final tug, and his foot came loose. Smith was now buried almost to his hips.

I should run, Diego thought. But he didn't.

Instead he crept down the bank, testing each patch of sand with his foot before he put his weight on it. He could feel the breeze from Smith's waving arms as he passed within inches of him and grabbed the rifle.

"Good boy," Smith said. "Hold on to one end and I'll grab the other. You're strong. You can pull me out."

Diego scrambled back up the bank. He turned and pointed the rifle at Smith.

One shot, and it would be over. No nightmares, no voices in the dark. And no one would know. One dead gringo, and Mando's death avenged.

"Now, that's not right, Diego. That's not respectful. After all I've done, I deserve some respect."

Diego closed his ears to the stupid words coming out of Smith's stupid mouth, but he couldn't silence his own heart. Killing Smith would be easy. It might even be right. But he couldn't do it.

He tossed the gun as far as he could into the water. It splashed, sank and disappeared. Then Diego took off into the shelter of the jungle.

"You think quicksand can kill me?" Smith bellowed after him. "Show me some respect!"

Diego kept running.

Too much had happened, and it had happened too fast. Diego needed not to think and not to feel. The rainforest towered around him.

For the rest of the day, Diego just walked. When the sun went back down and it was too dark to see, he dropped to the ground and fell asleep right there. If something wanted to eat him during the night, he didn't really care.

CHAPTER SIXTEEN

❊

Diego slept a long, deep, dreamless sleep, waking up to birds singing at the rising of the sun. He was stiff, bug-bitten, and his mouth was dry with thirst, but he was alive.

He moved himself slowly, feeling the aches. The canopy of leaves above him was green and glorious, and he was small against the ferns, insignificant among the trees that grew and grew, right up to heaven. Diego wondered if maybe he should just stay where he was. It was as good a place as any to wait to die.

A branch above him began to sway. He wiped a grimy hand over his eyes and saw a group of monkeys bouncing in the branches.

They howled, showed their teeth and threw things down at him – sticks, leaves, and fruit.

A banana landed not far from Diego. He picked it up. Although it was still mostly green, it was food. He unpeeled it and shoved it in his mouth. He looked around for other things the monkeys threw, and found two more bananas. One was already peeled. He wiped the dirt from it and swallowed it down.

The good sleep had cleared his head, and the food gave him back some of his strength. He stretched to get the ache out of his back, then started walking again. There was food in the jungle. And, somewhere, there was water.

There were many things in the jungle that could kill him, but there were many things that could keep him alive, too. After all, people had lived in the Amazon jungle long before cities, hotels and prisons even existed.

"Maybe I'll build myself a home here," Diego said to the monkeys. "I'll live off bananas, and hunt capybaras, and build a beautiful house for my family to live in when they get out of prison." A flock of brilliant red and orange parrots flew by him, and he took that to be a good sign.

Diego wondered briefly if Smith's men would come after him, and decided they probably wouldn't. They had the coca paste, and he didn't think any of them liked their boss enough to go wandering in the jungle looking for him.

As he walked, he planned the house he would build. It would be on stilts, but higher than the village houses, right up into the trees. Corina's screeching would scare away the snakes. He'd have his own room, with a door he could close to keep Corina out. His father would make furniture out of tree branches, and his mother would knit blankets out of vines.

The forest thinned, grew thick again, then opened up at a small watering hole on the edge of a meadow. A pair of giant otters rolled around each other in the pond. Diego was about to go down to the water's edge for a drink when he noticed a wild boar coming out of the brush, big tusks jutting out of the side of its face. Diego stuck to the edge of the trees, moving slowly so he wouldn't attract the boar's attention. Then he started to cross the clearing.

A meadow rose up around him in great moving clouds of color. Giant blue butterflies, smaller ones of red and yellow, others with bright purple wings flew up out of the grass as he walked through. Diego laughed, and the sound of his laughter seemed to draw out even more butterflies. They landed on his head, on his arms, on his shirt, before flying away again.

When the butterflies had settled back down, Diego looked around and saw the tops of hills rising out of the forest some distance away. If he could climb to the top of one of them, maybe he'd be able to spot a road or a village.

It was hard to continue in a straight line once he was back among the trees. There were too many things to avoid, like stands of nettles, and too many things to go around, like giant logs that were too big and mossy to climb over. For a long while, Diego worried that he was going off-course. Then the ground started to slope upward.

The thick vegetation started to thin out a bit, and the trees grew farther apart. There were tree stumps here and there.

Someone had cut firewood. That meant people might not be far away. Diego caught a hint of a fresh breeze. He went toward it.

The more he climbed, the more the forest fell

away. After several hours, he noticed a change in the temperature. The sun was hanging low in the sky. Night was coming. The sweat cooled on his body, and he began to shake with chill.

The trees gave way to bushes that were not much taller than he was. He recognized the little green leaves. They were the ones he had been stomping on for weeks.

Diego started pulling leaves off the bush branches and stuffing them in his mouth. The moisture in the leaves hit his throat like a prayer.

He picked and chewed, and for awhile he felt almost safe and almost happy. He'd spend the night under a coca bush, and Pachamama's gift would protect him.

"Those are our leaves," a female voice behind him said.

Diego jumped and spun around, a mouthful of green spit spurting out and running down his face and shirt. As he turned, his ribs hit the barrel of a very old rifle that was pointed at his belly. The other end of the gun was held by a girl, a little younger and a little smaller, with dark braids hanging down almost to the top of her jeans. On her face was a frown.

Diego was so relieved that he ignored the frown and started to brush past the gun until she stuck him hard in the chest with it.

"Those are our leaves," she said again. "Spit them out."

Diego did as he was told, making even more of a mess of himself in the process.

"My name is Diego," he said.

"Thief," the girl replied.

"Thief?" Diego looked down at himself, shook his head and laughed. "If I'm a thief, I'm not very good at it."

Not letting up one bit on her frown, the girl motioned with her head that he should start walking. The rifle moved from his chest to his back. Whenever he started to take a wrong turn, she hit him on the shoulder and set him right.

Diego didn't care. He could have run and escaped, but he knew the girl wouldn't kill him. He had seen that her clothes were clean, which meant there was water nearby, and very likely there would be food, too.

Before long, he caught the scent of wood fire and farm animals, and a sound of something that he hadn't heard in a long, long time – children laughing.

The bushes gave way to a clearing with a small stone and wood hut, just like the one he had shared with his parents. Smoke was rising from the chimney. Diego saw other wisps of smoke coming up behind the trees. There were neighbors.

A woman and man were playing a gentle game of kick ball with two small children. They looked up when a little dog barked and ran toward Diego and the girl, its tail wagging in welcome.

The woman was the first to reach them. She spoke in rapid Quechua. The girl reluctantly lowered the gun, and Diego's chilled arms were wrapped in the woman's shawl.

Almost before he knew it, he was sitting inside by the fire, with a mug of coca leaf tea in his hands.

It was as if he had stepped back in time. This house was a little bigger than his old one, but it had the same low ceilings, the same comfortable fire, the same smells from the potato and bean stew simmering on the grill. This could be his old house, his parents, his little sister on the floor making funny faces at him.

"We are the Ricardo family," the father said. "What is your name?"

"Diego Juárez."

"He's a thief," the older daughter said, standing with her arms folded across her chest. "I think we should shoot him."

"How can we shoot him, Bonita, when we have no bullets? You should throw that old gun back into the forest where you found it," the woman said. "Besides, look at his legs and hands. What do you see?"

"Dirt," Bonita said.

Diego tried to cover up his grimy legs with his grimy hands. Even through the dirt, they could see the bleached white skin and the blisters from the chemicals.

"He's been in the pits," Mrs. Ricardo said. "And if he's up here, lost and on his own, then something bad must have happened. Am I right?"

Diego felt his face tighten. He didn't want to cry in front of the girl with the gun, but stopping the tears made his face hurt. He replied with a simple nod.

"A mean business attracts mean people," the father said. "Where are you from, son?"

"Cochabamba," Diego managed to say.

"So you left the city with the promise of riches beyond belief, and now here you are."

"It's time to eat, not time to lecture," Mrs. Ricardo said, putting a bowl of stew in Diego's hands. "Where are your parents?"

"San Sebastián."

The man and woman nodded. "Many from this area are guests of the good saint," the woman said, dishing up food for the rest of the family. "If he were alive today, I wonder how he would feel about his holy name hanging over a prison."

Diego ate. There wasn't much food in his bowl, but it was hot, and it felt warm and good in the great hole that was his stomach.

Truly safe for the first time in a long while, exhaustion was hitting him hard.

He struggled to keep his eyes open, but his eyelids were too heavy. Mrs. Ricardo took his empty bowl from him.

"Talk is for tomorrow," she said. "Sleep is for tonight."

He felt Mr. Ricardo's strong arms lift him gently to a soft bed. A blanket covered him, and he sank into a deep, safe place.

He would sleep tonight, rise with the sun, and be ready in the morning for whatever came next.

AUTHOR'S NOTE

Bolivia is the poorest country in South America and the second-poorest in the Western hemisphere, after Haiti. It is a land-locked nation of breathtaking geographic diversity, including the Andes Mountains, high rocky plains and the dense lowland rainforests of the Amazon basin.

For thousands of years, communities of peoples have made their home there, including the great civilizations of the Tiahuanaco and the Inca. In the 1500s, the Spanish conquistadors left their mark on Bolivia as they had in much of the rest of South America.

In 1544, a rich vein of silver was discovered in the city of Potosí — enough to enrich two hundred years of Spanish monarchs and nobles. Untold numbers of

African slaves and indigenous workers suffered in horrific conditions to extract the silver. Many died. The mountain is still mined today, and many of the miners are children.

The Spanish found that workers who chewed the little green coca leaf worked longer, since coca takes away pain and hunger. They encouraged its widespread use, even paying their workers with coca leaves. At the same time, European missionaries condemned the use of coca as part of their cultural war against indigenous traditions.

Coca is still used on a daily basis by many Bolivians. The leaves are chewed and are also made into a tea. It eases living and working at high altitudes. Coca tea is even served at the U.S. embassy in La Paz. For many Bolivian indigenous people, coca is a sacred plant used in religious rituals.

Cocaine was first created from coca in 1860 by a German scientist named Albert Nieman. It quickly gained popularity in the industrialized world as a legal stimulant and painkiller, and it was an ingredient in the original formula of Coca-Cola.

The U.S. Congress passed the first restrictions on cocaine in 1914, but the drug rose in popularity in the 1960s and 70s, initially among wealthy people looking for amusement. Later, in its cheaper form as crack cocaine, it flooded communities of disadvantaged people who were looking for a way to escape daily poverty and pain.

A "War on Drugs" was declared by U.S. President Richard Nixon in 1968. Over the next decades, this led to military incursions targeting indigenous growers and the propping up of corrupt regimes with appalling human rights records. It did not lead to a reduction of cocaine entering the United States.

The coca farmers in Bolivia organized themselves into a union after their crops were destroyed by the government, leaving them without an income. In 2005, after many short-lived governments, the Bolivian people elected Evo Morales, the first-ever indigenous president of the country, and leader of the coca growers (cocaleros). The cocalero movement is based on retaining the growing of coca, finding further uses for the coca leaf, and on respect for the sacred and cultural importance of coca.

GLOSSARY

Aguayo – A large, colorful cloth.

Altiplano – High plain that stretches across Bolivia.

Anticuchos – Chunks of meat and potato roasted on skewers.

Aymara – Group of indigenous people who live in the Andean region of South America, mainly in Bolivia. Also the traditional language of the Aymara.

Boliviano – Bolivian money.

Bombo – Bolivian drum.

Campesino – Farmer; peasant.

Capybara – Giant brown rodent related to the guinea pig.

Centavo – Bolivian money; there are one hundred centavos in a Boliviano.

Chicha – Alcoholic drink made from corn or other local plants.

Chichería – Place that makes and sells chicha.

Chupe – Soup containing meat, grains and vegetables.

Coca – Small shrub grown in the Andes. Its leaves have been used by the indigenous people of the Andes for centuries for food, medicine and religious rituals.

Cocaine – Illegal drug made from coca leaves that have been processed into paste.

Cocalero – Coca farmer.

Gringo – Slang for a citizen of the United States.

Inca – Citizens of the Inca Empire, which was centered in Peru.

K'guaka – Aymara for "How much?"

Legia – Clump of potato or quínoa ash chewed with coca leaves.

Loco – Crazy.

Milanesa – Thin piece of breaded meat.

Narco – Drug dealer.

Pachamama – Aymara term for Mother Earth.

Paya – Aymara for the number two.

Quechua – Language spoken by people who live in certain parts of the Andean region, including

Bolivia. People who speak Quechua are often called Quechua.

Quimsa – Aymara for the number three.

Quínoa – Very nutritious food plant grown in the Andes, ground and used as cereal.

Saltenas – Pastry stuffed with meat and vegetables.

Sanka – Musical instrument made of long bamboo pipes of various lengths lashed together.

Tienda – Small shop selling groceries and basic household goods.

Trufti – Minibus.

Yatiri – Aymara word for a wise learned person.

ABOUT THE AUTHOR

DEBORAH ELLIS has achieved international acclaim with her courageous, sensitive and dramatic books that give Western readers a glimpse into the plight of children in developing countries. Her Breadwinner trilogy has sold hundreds of thousands of copies in seventeen languages. She has won the Governor General's Award, Sweden's Peter Pan Prize, the Ruth Schwartz Award, the University of California's Middle East Book Award and the Jane Addams' Peace Award. She lives in Simcoe, Ontario.

COMING SOON
THE SEQUEL TO
I AM A TAXI –

SACRED LEAF
by Deborah Ellis

A terrible sound reached Diego's ears as he straightened himself up from the patch of sweet potatoes he was weeding.

Only one thing could make such a noise.

And then it was upon them, giant and green, propellers thumping as it hovered over the small farm.

The little ones screamed and started to run. Mrs. Ricardo snatched them up in her arms, went down on her knees and turned their wailing faces to her chest to shield them from the flying debris stirred up by the propellers. Diego watched as drying coca leaves took to the air like butterflies and scattered to the four winds.

The helicopter landed in the family's yard. At the same time, a pick-up truck sped up the dirt road. Soldiers spilled out, pointing their weapons and trampling the vegetable gardens under their heavy boots. The propellers slowed to a halt, and for a moment there was silence in the clearing as the soldiers and the family stared at each other.

Then there was a horrible yell, and Diego saw Bonita run out of the hut, her old, useless rifle pointed at the soldiers around the helicopter. Diego heard the soldiers step forward, heard them raise their rifles to firing position...

Hardcover: 0-88899-751-5
$18.95 CDN / $16.95 US

Paperback: 0-88899-808-2
$9.95 CDN / $6.95 US

To be published by Groundwood Books in Fall 2007.